T5-CVF-628

About the size of a large monkey, the creature had a short, stocky body covered with greenish-gray fur. Its oversized head sported two big, shiny eyes like huge black marbles, and its face had a weird, reptilian look, kind of like that of an angry monster. To Anne, the creature looked like one of the hideous gargoyles that adorned the roof of the old cathedral in the center of town.

What is that horrible thing? she wanted to shout, then she quickly remembered that she was invisible.

But almost as if it had heard her shout anyway, the creature suddenly turned Anne's way and locked its huge black eyes with her green ones. Then, moving with catlike speed, it leaped up on its short but powerful legs and raised its crooked arms to reveal a pair of talonlike claws.

OTHER BOOKS BY ALLEN B. URY

SCARY MYSTERIES FOR SLEEP-OVERS

MORE SCARY MYSTERIES FOR SLEEP-OVERS

SCARY STORIES FOR SLEEP-OVERS (A NOVEL)
Lost in Horror Valley

SCARY STORIES FOR WHEN YOU'RE HOME ALONE

MORE SCARY STORIES FOR WHEN YOU'RE HOME ALONE

BITES
A Fate Worse Than Death &
More Fright with a Bite

The Hunt &
More Fright with a Bite

HOWL
The 13th Room &
Other Tales of Full-Moon Madness

The Boy Who Cried Werewolf &
Other Tales of Full-Moon Madness

CRAWLERS
Books 1—4

THE LIVING GHOST

Copyright © 1996 by RGA Publishing Group, Inc.
All rights reserved. No part of this work may be
reproduced or transmitted in any form or by any means,
electronic or mechanical, including photocopying and
recording, or by any information storage or retrieval
system, except as may be expressly permitted by the
1976 Copyright Act or in writing by the publisher.

ISBN: 1-56565-520-6

Library of Congress Catalog Card Number: 96-2986

Publisher: Jack Artenstein
General Manager, Juvenile Division: Elizabeth Amos
Director of Publishing Services: Rena Copperman
Editor in Chief of Fiction, Juvenile Division: Barbara Schoichet
Managing Editor, Juvenile Division: Lindsey Hay
Art Director: Lisa-Theresa Lenthall
Designer: Cheryl Carrington

Lowell House books can be purchased at special discounts
when ordered in bulk for premiums and special sales.
Contact Department JH at the following address:

Lowell House Juvenile
2029 Century Park East, Suite 3290
Los Angeles, CA 90067

Manufactured in the United States of America

10 9 8 7 6 5 4 3 2 1

A NOVEL

SCARY STORIES

THE LIVING GHOST

ALLEN B. URY

Lowell House
Juvenile
Los Angeles

CONTEMPORARY BOOKS
Chicago

For Rene,
who makes all things possible
—A.B.U.

CHAPTER ONE

Anne Felcher scanned her bedroom, looking for signs of movement. Sliding her painter's easel aside, she walked cautiously over to where her eighth grade class picture lay on the carpet. She'd been working on her painting—a self-portrait—when suddenly the framed photograph fell off the shelf, seemingly all by itself.

"Hmm, I wonder what could have caused that," she mumbled, nervously clutching her grandmother's ivory cameo necklace. She'd recently begun wearing it for good luck. The way the picture had suddenly fallen, it was as though some strong, invisible hand had swatted it off the shelf, leaving everything else completely untouched.

She was just about to bend down and pick up the picture, when all at once she felt a slight breeze blow against the back of her neck. It lifted her shoulder-length blond hair and sent a chill down her spine. *That's odd*, she thought, realizing that she'd felt the exact same breeze brush by her neck just before the picture had fallen.

Startled, Anne looked around her bedroom for the source of the breeze. The door was closed. The windows were shut. She glanced up at the air vent over the door frame, and got up on her tiptoes to feel if the heat was on. But no air was coming out.

"Must have been a tiny earthquake," she told herself, though she knew she hadn't felt even the slightest tremor. Then, deciding to dismiss the whole thing, she quickly knelt down to retrieve the fallen picture. She was anxious to get back to her painting. She'd just finished working on the bridge of her thin, tapered nose, and was about to move on to what she considered the hardest thing for an artist to capture—the eyes.

But when Anne turned over the frame, her chest tightened and her blood ran cold. The glass had cracked, forming an eerie spiderweb across the photo, and the center of the web was directly over *her* face!

Her hands trembling, Anne held the picture flat to avoid dropping bits of broken glass. Then she headed downstairs to the kitchen where her mother, home from her part-time bookkeeping job, was preparing dinner.

"Mom, look what happened," Anne said, setting the shattered picture on the countertop.

"How'd you do that?" her mother gasped.

"I didn't," Anne replied. "I was working on my painting when it fell off my bookshelf and broke."

"Well, it's really no problem," her mother said. She pulled a paper garbage bag out from under the sink, lifted the damaged picture off the counter, then shook the loose glass shards into the bag. "There. The picture's fine. I can get a new piece of glass at the art store tomorrow."

But Anne was still troubled. "Mom, I think there was something in my room," she said anxiously. "I think it intentionally knocked the picture off. I could just, well, *sense* it."

"So what are you saying?" her mother asked. "That there was a ghost in your room? Oh, Anne, don't be silly!"

"I know it sounds silly," Anne admitted. "But I've seen shows about this kind of thing. You know, objects moving across tables and glasses flying through the air. And these things were reported by grown-ups—*not* kids."

Anne's mother rolled her eyes and sighed. "How many times have I told you, don't believe everything you see on TV. A lot of those ghost stories are told by people who just want to get attention. Either that, or the shows' producers take advantage of these poor people, who actually believe they've seen a ghost, just to get high ratings."

"Well, *I'm* not trying to get attention," Anne countered. "So how do you explain what I just felt in my room?"

Her mother smiled. "Look, sweetheart. I'm not a scientist like your father, but I know enough about how the world works to assure you, *there are no ghosts.* Now, how about helping me by making the salad for tonight? It'll help bring your mind back to the real world."

But while Anne tore lettuce, cut tomatoes, grated carrots, chopped radishes, and sliced cucumbers, her mind kept wandering back to the falling picture and the odd breeze she'd felt just before the glass was shattered. Then she recalled all the other odd incidents that had happened recently around the house. Like the time she'd set her schoolbooks on her desk, stepped briefly from her room, then returned to find them scattered all over the floor. Or the time the washing machine had started up, and no one was doing laundry. And then there was the time the garage door kept opening and closing for no apparent reason.

Her parents had blamed the family cat for the washing machine incident, suggesting that the fat tabby had stepped on one of the control buttons. And they'd said that a faulty remote control was responsible for the problem with the garage door. But Anne had been giving the cat a bath when the washing machine started acting up, and when the garage door service man had checked out the remote, all he did was change the batteries. Could there have been another, more sinister explanation for all this weirdness? After her class photo had fallen, Anne was pretty sure that there was.

But before she went off the deep end and began a ghost hunt, Anne decided to talk to her father. Maybe he could come up with some kind of scientific reasons that would explain everything away. If he couldn't, Anne was ready to tell her parents they'd better start looking for a new home—because this one was haunted!

Anne's dad, Dr. Benjamin Felcher, was a physicist at Johnston & MacNamara Laboratories just outside of their hometown of Locklear, California. The lab was one of those fancy ultra-high-tech places where men and women in white lab coats developed lasers, supercomputers, and other technologies that used to be found only in science fiction books.

But lucky for Anne, her dad didn't always have to relate everything to science. In fact, he was a man who liked stupid comedy movies and rock music as much as electrophysics and differential calculus.

Because of this, Anne felt she could count on her father to approach just about any subject with an open mind—even offbeat subjects like ghosts. Still, when she brought up the subject that night at the dining room table, her dad's reaction was not nearly as accepting as she would have hoped.

"Forget it, Anne. There are no ghosts. Dead is dead. The end of the line. No deposit, no return," he said glibly. Then he grinned. "Now, if you're asking me if there are unusual phenomena that science cannot yet explain, then yes, there may be forces out there that *act* like ghosts. I mean, come on, we'd be fools to believe that we know *everything* there is to know and that we've identified *all* of nature's laws." He raised a quizzical eyebrow. "But the more interesting question is, why are you concerned about ghosts all of a sudden?"

Now feeling slightly foolish, Anne described what had happened in her bedroom that afternoon. Her dad listened carefully for a few moments, then offered his own explanation.

"An earth tremor," he said flatly.

"I already thought of that," Anne replied. "But I didn't feel an earthquake. And there weren't any reported. I checked the papers and watched the five o'clock news."

"Here in California, hundreds of minor earthquakes occur every week, none of which are big enough to make the news," her father said. "Anyway, if it wasn't an earth tremor, then it was probably just a vibration from a passing truck. Or maybe it was just a low-flying airplane. But, believe me, Anne, it wasn't a—"

Just then, Anne's glass fell over. For a moment, Anne and her parents just stared at the puddle of milk as it spread across the tablecloth.

"Did you see that?" Anne finally managed to ask. "My hands were nowhere near that glass!"

"Another earth tremor," her father said with complete confidence in his voice.

"Well, I'd better clean that up," her mother said.

"No, I'll do it," Anne said, quickly getting up and heading into the kitchen. She needed to be alone for a few minutes to collect her thoughts. Whether her parents believed it or not, something was in the house with them, and it was desperately trying to get their attention.

Now standing at the sink, her mind racing, Anne turned on the tap to moisten a sponge when she felt something move in back of her. Spinning around, she scanned the room. But there was nothing there.

Shuddering, she turned back to the sink to turn off the water when suddenly a thundering spray of water shot out of the faucet. Anne shrieked as the water splashed all over her shirt, and then, to her amazement, the faucet turned off . . . all by itself!

"Honey, what's wrong?" her mother called.

"N-n-nothing, Mom," Anne stammered, unable to take her eyes off the faucet. How could she tell her mother that the faucet had just attacked her? That she'd once again felt an unseen presence in the room? Her dad had said there was no such thing as ghosts, but if ghosts didn't exist, then what *was* invading their home?

CHAPTER TWO

The next day, Anne couldn't wait to tell her best friends, Judy Slocum and Kara Winowski, about the odd goings-on at her house. She sat impatiently through all her morning classes, then, when the lunch bell finally rang, she headed straight for the cafeteria to the table near the vending machines where they always sat.

But no sooner had Anne arrived at their table than Judy, a tireless motormouth, began talking away at a hundred miles per hour.

"Anne, did you hear the news?" she said giddily. "Crystal Norberg dumped Tony Gilette! Can you believe it? Those two have been going together for, like, *forever!*"

"I don't believe it!" Anne gasped, all thoughts of ghosts and haunted houses disappearing from her brain. "Crystal's got to be crazy!"

Like most of the girls at Thomas Jefferson Junior High, Anne thought Tony was handsome enough to be a movie star, and she'd have given her left lung just to go out for ice cream with the guy. But Tony only had eyes for Crystal Norberg, a tall, green-eyed blond with a supermodel body, so it had been pointless to do anything but admire Tony from afar. Now Anne could barely sit still. If Judy was right, if Tony was suddenly available, then maybe *she* actually had a chance.

"Details, Judy," Anne cried. "I want to hear every single detail!"

"Are you guys talking about Tony and Crystal?" Kara asked, approaching the table with a lunch tray that was practically empty. Kara, a heavyset girl with frizzy brown hair, thick horn-rimmed glasses, and a lively sense of humor, always was on a diet but never seemed to lose a pound. "I heard they just—"

"Fashion Police! Fashion Police!" someone suddenly cried from a nearby table. It was Lisa Connors, a slim brunette with a heart-shaped face and piercing brown eyes. As usual, Lisa was dressed in the latest designer fashions, as were the other three girls in her exclusive "clique." Infamous for looking down on kids who didn't measure up to her personal standards of beauty, breeding, and good taste, Lisa was now pointing at Kara who had had the nerve to wear a pair of striped pants that were "in" last year, but totally "out" now. "Give that girl ten years with no possibility of parole!"

"Oh, bug off, Lisa!" Anne shot back, fed up by Lisa's unrelenting snootiness. "The only place you've got taste is in your mouth!"

Lisa reacted with pretend shock, then broke out into a wicked smile. "That's pretty good, Felcher," she said. "I like a girl who sticks up for her friends. It shows real courage. And I respect that. Tell you what, dessert's on me today!" With that, she rose and headed over to the vending machines at the back of the cafeteria.

"Hmm, I wonder what *she's* up to?" Judy asked suspiciously. "I wouldn't trust her for a minute, if I were you."

Anne shrugged. "Who cares? Lisa's a stuck-up jerk." She took a bite of her sliced turkey sandwich, then turned to Kara. "She had no right to talk to you like that, Kara. Besides, I think your clothes are, uh, kind of original."

Kara picked up a carrot stick and eyed it mournfully. "I wish *I* could eat a dessert," she said, looking at her ample hips. "Don't you think these stripes make me look—"

But before she could finish her sentence, Hillary Tyler, one of the girls at Lisa's table, screamed, "A cockroach!" and jumped to her feet. A tall, athletic girl who wore her light brown hair tied back in a pony tail, Hillary was the star of the girls' volleyball team, and when she jumped, people noticed.

Instantly, Anne, Judy, Kara, and just about everyone around leapt to their feet and began scanning the area for the insect invader. Then suddenly Hillary put her hands in the air and offered an embarrassed grin to everyone. "Sorry," she announced. "It was just a raisin."

With that, everyone let out a collective groan, then went back to their lunches.

"What a jerk," Kara groaned, as she plopped back heavily into her seat.

"She probably needs glasses, but she's too vain to wear them," Judy noted.

Wondering how loud Hillary would have screamed if she'd been visited by a *ghost,* Anne fell back into her chair, when suddenly something gooey, cold, and wet squished beneath her.

"Ahhhh!" she screamed.

Leaping back up, Anne looked down at her chair and saw the flattened remains of a huge slice of banana cream pie.

"I guess I was wrong," Lisa Connors said, as she suddenly appeared behind Anne's chair. "Dessert's not on me—it's on *you!*"

With that, Lisa and all her friends began to laugh uproariously. Then the other kids around her started laughing as well, pointing at the whipped cream and meringue still clinging to the back of Anne's skirt.

Anne blushed with embarrassment and her green eyes welled up with tears as waves of laughter burst forth from all the other tables. All she wanted to do was disappear. To vanish. To make herself invisible and get as far away from this school and Lisa Connors as she possibly could.

But Anne knew that she didn't have that option, and so she quickly gathered up her books and ran out of the cafeteria, leaving globs of whipped cream and meringue, and bits of pie crust in her wake.

"That should teach her a lesson," Lisa said as she and her friends exchanged a series of triumphant high-fives.

"All of you make me sick," Judy said, a look of disgust on her face.

"I think I've lost my appetite," Kara said, pushing her tray away. Then together, the two girls rose and marched out of the cafeteria to find their friend and console her.

"Oh, please!" shouted Rita Wallace, another of Lisa's cohorts, whose makeup was always done just right to accentuate her freckles and red hair. "Can't any of you guys appreciate a good prank when you see one? I mean, really! You guys don't have *any* sense of humor!"

"Forget about them," Lisa said with a sneer, her almond eyes narrowing into reptilian slits. "If you think that was a good little prank, just wait until you see what else I've got cooking inside my brain for Miss Anne Felcher. No, I'm not quite finished with her yet."

Judy and Kara found Anne sitting on the school's front steps gazing at her most prized possession— the ivory cameo that hung from a delicate beaded chain around her neck.

"Don't let Lisa and her stupid friends get to you," Judy advised, sitting beside Anne. "They're just a bunch of stuck-up snobs, and everyone in the whole school knows it."

"Hey, did you ever hear the expression, 'Don't get mad, get even'?" Kara asked, sitting down on Anne's other side. "How about we give Lisa Connors a taste of her own medicine?"

"Are you suggesting that we play a practical joke on *her?*" Anne asked.

"Exactly," Kara said with a twinkle in her eyes and a mischievious grin. "When she's preoccupied with something, we could glue her books together. Or put itching powder in her gym shorts!"

Anne considered what fun it would be to get back at Lisa . . . until she considered the revenge Lisa would surely take on her.

"No," Anne finally replied. "That would just be stooping to Lisa's level, and I won't do that."

"Okay, I guess I wouldn't either," Judy reluctantly agreed. "I forgot. Nothing's more dangerous than a wounded animal."

The girls sat in awkward silence for several seconds. Then Kara noticed Anne's cameo. "Hey, nice necklace," she said, eager to change the subject. "Where'd you get it?"

"It belonged to my grandmother. She died over two years ago, and willed it to me, but my mom wouldn't let me wear it until recently since it's so delicate," Anne explained, holding the intricately carved cameo up for her friends to see. The piece featured a side view of a young, nineteenth century woman sculpted out of ivory.

"Can I try it on?" Judy asked. "I promise to be extra careful with it."

Anne shook her head. "Sorry, it's nothing against you personally, it's just that my mother made me promise never to let anyone else wear it. You see, my grandmother had it on until the day she died. Now, when I wear the cameo, I imagine that her spirit is watching over me."

"Well, it's beautiful," Kara said with a sigh. "Too bad your grandmother's spirit can't come back and give Lisa Connors a good scare!"

Just then the bell rang, signaling lunch was over.

"Oh, this is just great," Anne muttered. "Now I get to walk around smelling like a banana cream pie and watch everyone laughing at the goo all over the back of my skirt."

Miraculously, Anne not only managed to get through the rest of her day, but things actually got better. In fact, that afternoon her science teacher, Mr. Gallway, made a surprise announcement.

"Next Wednesday we're all going on a field trip to the Johnston & MacNamara Laboratories," he said. "We'll see some of the breakthroughs being made in computers, medical science, robotics, and other fields. We'll also get to talk to the scientists who are behind these remarkable advancements, including the father of our own Anne Felcher. Dr. Felcher is one of Johnston & MacNamara's top scientists! Isn't that right, Anne?"

Flushing with pride and embarrassment, Anne couldn't have been happier. All of a sudden, everyone in her science class wanted to talk to her, to get the inside track on what was going on at her father's lab. At least for the next week, she was destined to be even more popular than snob extraordinaire Lisa Connors or beauty queen Crystal Norberg, both of whom knew about as much about high-energy physics as a toad.

And so, although she smelled like a tropical fruit and looked like she needed to take a shower—with her clothes on!—Anne had a relatively pleasant rest of the day.

"Guess what, Dad," Anne said excitedly over dinner that night. "We're going to take a field trip to your lab next Wednesday."

"I know," her dad replied with a twinkle in his eye. "You'll be there just in time to watch us test our new photon refraction field."

"Your *what?*" Anne asked, grimacing like what he said didn't taste good.

"It's a system for selectively bending light," her father explained. "The Department of Defense is very interested in this new technology, not only for making airplanes invisible while in flight, but also for camouflaging troops on the ground."

"That sounds wild," Anne said enthusiastically. "How does it work?"

"It's hard to explain," he confessed. "I'm not even sure I understand it all. Let's just say that it takes a lot of energy and a very fancy computer that makes your state-of-the-art desktop model look like an old-fashioned adding machine."

"You're actually going to let the *kids* watch the test?" Anne's mother asked in disbelief. "Shouldn't a test like that be top-secret?"

"The Cold War's over, honey," Dr. Felcher gently reminded her. "Besides, if the test goes off as I hope it does, the kids will see, well, absolutely nothing!"

Dr. Felcher couldn't help but laugh at his own joke. Anne and her mother laughed, too. But none of them would have so much as chuckled if they'd known what was going to happen next.

CHAPTER THREE

"And this is our main data processing center," said Ms. Roebuck, the cheerful research assistant who'd been assigned to take Anne's class on its tour of the lab. "This mainframe computer has a storage capacity of over two million gigabytes, and can process up to a billion computations every second."

She gestured to a large, off-white machine that looked like an industrial refrigerator. Except for a few blinking lights that showed the computer was operating, its face was absolutely featureless.

"Kind of makes our home computers look like old-fashioned adding machines," Anne quipped, repeating her father's words from the week before.

"Exactly," Ms. Roebuck said with a sugary grin. "Now, if you'll follow me, we'll move on to Area Six, the largest laboratory in the complex. Remember, no food or drinks are allowed beyond this point."

With Anne in the lead, the thirty eighth-graders and their teacher marched down a series of twisting halls to the secured doorway that led to the lab. Everyone was so busy being impressed by the building's futuristic architecture and high-tech security features that no one saw the can of soda Hillary Tyler was hiding under her designer jacket.

A few minutes later, they entered a massive, thirty-foot-high room that looked like the inside of a huge water tank. One half of the room was occupied by a large electronic control center, which stood on a raised platform. Above this control center was a glass-walled observation booth. Below it was what looked like a large metal shed about the size of a two-car garage. This structure was surrounded by a number of tanks, pipes, and power conduits, all of which looked very complicated and very, *very* dangerous.

"Wow!" several people said, as everyone turned around gazing at the various levels of the chamber itself, all of which were joined by an interconnecting series of metal staircases and walkways.

"Come on, kids," Ms. Roebuck said with a wave of her arm as she led the eager group down two flights of stairs to the front of the garagelike enclosure on the lowest level. There was only one small entrance to this room, which now stood wide open. As instructed, the students stepped through the doorway one by one until they were all inside.

"This is the chamber where the experiment will be conducted," Ms. Roebuck explained. "The room's walls, floors, and ceiling are lined with thin strips of metal which will carry enough electricity to create the photon refraction field our scientists are hoping to perfect." She pointed to a black, rectangular metal pedestal in the center of the room. It stood about four feet tall and two feet wide, and sitting on top of it was a clear, basketball-sized package of electronic instruments. "The package on top of that pedestal holds over a hundred sensors designed to transmit data back to our central computer," Ms. Roebuck went on, the same plastic smile frozen on her perfectly made-up face. "If all goes well, when the refraction field reaches full strength, the entire package should disappear."

"You mean, it'll disintegrate?" Judy Slocum asked.

"No, it will still be here," Ms. Roebuck replied. "It just won't be visible to the human eye." She went on to explain some of the basic physical theories behind the experiment, but none of the kids seemed to pay much attention. Even their science teacher, Mr. Gallway, who had the reputation for knowing everything there was to know about science, wore a blank, faraway look.

Near the back of the room, Hillary Tyler, who looked just as confused as the rest of the class, took the opportunity to sneak a sip from her hidden soda can. As she did, she was accidentally elbowed in the side by a fidgety boy standing next to her. For a moment, she lost her grip on the can, and at least an ounce of the drink spilled onto the floor.

"You stupid—" But Hillary caught herself, deciding to let it go rather than call attention to the soda she wasn't supposed to have anyway.

At the same time, Lisa Connors and Rita Wallace were coldly eyeing Anne, who stood just a few feet away, unconsciously fingering her beloved cameo.

"What's with that necklace she's always wearing lately?" Lisa whispered to her friend.

"Some kind of antique," Rita whispered back. "I hear it came from her grandmother or something."

"Gee, it would be a shame if she lost it, wouldn't it?" Lisa said with a mischievous smile. "I bet it would just break her little heart."

"It sure would," Rita agreed, understanding Lisa's message loud and clear.

As Ms. Roebuck continued to drone on and on, Lisa and Rita slowly worked their way through the crowd until they were positioned on either side of Anne. No sooner had they arrived than a siren sounded and a yellow warning light flashed overhead.

"That's the signal for us to leave," Ms. Roebuck announced, ushering everyone toward the door. "The countdown has started. Let's all move into the visitors' gallery."

Like kids hurrying to board a theme park thrill ride, the students began filing quickly out of the test chamber. Anne, in the middle of the pack, moved along with the others, until Rita "accidentally" blocked her way.

"Oops, I didn't see you." Rita said apologetically.

While Rita spoke, Lisa withdrew a small pair of nail clippers from her purse, moved close up behind Anne, and quickly snipped her necklace in two. Anne, distracted by Rita and the surging crowd, didn't feel a thing, and was totally unaware that her precious cameo had fallen to the floor.

Moving single file, the students headed up a narrow metal staircase that led to a glass-enclosed observation room fifteen feet above the main floor. It was from here that they would watch the scientists conduct their bold experiment. Anne, who had now fallen back in the crowd, had just stepped into the observation room when she absentmindedly reached for her cameo . . . only to find it wasn't there!

"Oh, no!" she gasped, frantically scanning the floor. But when she saw no sign of the heirloom in the immediate area, she had to conclude that she'd dropped it somewhere between here and the refraction chamber.

"Excuse me . . . excuse me," Anne repeated, as she pressed against the flow of incoming kids, working her way back to the exit. Counting heads, Ms. Roebuck didn't even see Anne as she ducked behind her and headed out the door.

"I've got to find it," Anne muttered to herself as she quickly descended the metal staircase all the way down to the first floor walkway.

Now standing all alone outside the refraction chamber, Anne tried to decide what to do. Soon the room's vaultlike door would automatically swing shut and the experiment would begin. Was there enough time to look for the necklace? From the conversations Anne had had with her father, she knew enough about this test to know that she was looking at a safety window of mere seconds.

She could, of course, wait until the experiment was over and look for the cameo, but what if the invisibility effect was permanent? Then she'd never find the piece, even if it *was* in the chamber.

Sucking in a deep breath, she jumped through the doorway, and to her joy, instantly spotted the necklace lying on the floor, right behind the pedestal with the electronic instrument package on top. Without hesitation, Anne raced toward it . . . only to slip on the puddle of soda Hillary had spilled earlier.

"Whoa!" she yelped as she fell forward and hit her head on the corner of the support pillar.

Sinking to the floor, her head roaring with pain, Anne rubbed her right temple. "I've got to get out of . . ." she mumbled as she slumped to the floor behind the pedestal just as the chamber's heavy door swung closed and sealed itself with a dull *thunk*.

CHAPTER FOUR

In the main control room that overlooked the test chamber, Dr. Felcher supervised his crew of eight highly trained scientists and engineers as the photon refraction field test moved into its final, critical phase.

"Countdown stands at T-minus thirty seconds and counting," announced a middle-aged female technician with fiery red hair. She peered over her half-rimmed glasses to watch a series of numbers flash by on her computer monitor.

"We're already receiving various data from the instrument package, Dr. Felcher," said the man next to her, an Asian-born engineer who looked like he was just out of college. "Power is at eighty percent and climbing rapidly," he went on, adjusting a few of the instruments.

A quartet of monitor screens showed closed-circuit pictures of the spherical instrument package sitting within the test chamber. But all four of the cameras were positioned so as to show only the package itself, *not* the pedestal it sat on, and certainly not anything—or *anyone*—who might be lying unconscious on the chamber floor.

"Switch to automatic," Dr. Felcher ordered.

"Done," said another scientist, a short, balding man who clicked an icon on his computer screen with his mouse, then added, "The computer's in charge. We're committed and moving toward final countdown as we speak."

"We're at fifteen seconds," the red-haired woman reported, nervously twirling a pencil between her manicured fingers. "Everything's a go."

Above the main control room in the visitors' gallery, Anne's science teacher, Mr. Gallway, stood among his students, all of whom were crammed up against the glass, hoping to get a good view of whatever it was that was going on below. But the look on the teacher's face showed that he was definitely preoccupied and worried about something.

"Where's Anne Felcher?" he suddenly asked with alarm. "Has anyone seen her?"

"The last time I saw her, she was running back to the test chamber, Mr. Gallway," Kara Winowski volunteered. "She looked kind of —"

"She *what?*" Mr. Gallway gasped. He quickly turned to Ms. Roebuck, who was standing next to him, and grabbed her arm. "You've got to stop the test! Anne Felcher might be in that chamber!"

"That's impossible," Ms. Roebuck insisted. "I took a head count as everyone left. Maybe she's down in the control room with her father."

Mr. Gallway pushed a knot of students aside and dragged Ms. Roebuck over to the observation window. "Okay, where is she?" the science teacher demanded. "Do you see her down there?"

"M-maybe she's in the restroom," Ms. Roebuck suggested nervously, her cheerful attitude cracking for the first time. At the same moment, the countdown boomed over the booth's loudspeakers, "Three . . . two . . . one . . ."

In the sealed test chamber, Anne Felcher continued to lie unconscious as thousands of volts of electricity suddenly surged through the walls around her. Invisible to the human eye, the powerful energy fields expanded, then merged, recombining to form patterns unlike anything found in the natural world. These fields wrapped themselves around all the objects within the chamber—not to mention a single eighth-grader named Anne Felcher—and strange, miraculous changes began to take place.

Lost in the blackness of a dreamless sleep, Anne didn't see a thing when both the black rectangular pedestal and the globe-shaped instrument package on top of it began to shimmer, vibrate, and ripple as if deep within a desert mirage. She was also blissfully unaware when, a split second later, the objects completely disappeared from sight—and she disappeared along with them.

"Abort! Abort!" Dr. Felcher shouted to the stunned scientists seated before him. Only seconds before, Ms. Roebuck, her voice choked with panic, had telephoned from the observation booth to report that his daughter might be trapped inside the refraction field test chamber. Immediately, Dr. Felcher had checked the four monitors that displayed the chamber's interior, but they showed only an empty room. He knew, of course, that this proved nothing, since everything within the chamber was at this point invisible. There was only one way to tell if Anne was indeed in there, and that was to stop the experiment cold.

"But all our readings show that everything is—" an engineer began.

"I said abort!" Dr. Felcher bellowed. Then, not having time to explain, he lunged at the control panel and hit a large red button.

A moment later, the room was filled with the sound of generators winding down.

"Why did you do *that?*" the red-haired woman demanded, angrily whipping off her glasses.

"I think my daughter's in that chamber!" Dr. Felcher shouted, his eyes wild with panic. "I've got to get her out of there!"

Thundering down the metal stairs, Dr. Felcher ran as fast as he could to the test chamber. When he arrived at the large, vaultlike door, he hurriedly punched his personal pass code into a small digital keypad by the entrance. A moment later, there was the dull *thunk* of bolts being released, and the door automatically opened with a soft, mechanical hum.

Dashing into the chamber, Dr. Felcher found Anne lying motionless on the floor beside the now-visible instrument package's rectangular pedestal. Her hand was reaching toward her grandmother's cameo, which lay nearby.

Fearing the worst, he rushed to her side. "Anne!" he cried. Turning the unconscious girl over, he immediately saw an ugly purple welt on her right temple and a trickle of blood flowing down her cheek. He quickly checked Anne's neck for a pulse, and sighed with relief when he found his daughter's heartbeat steady and strong. "Anne, it's me," he whispered, stroking her hair. "Are you all right?"

"I—I'm very tired," Anne muttered.

"Dr. Felcher, is she . . ?" It was the red-headed technician. She and several of the other control room scientists stood crowded in the doorway, their faces white with fear.

"Get a medical team down here immediately," Dr. Felcher barked. "I want my daughter taken to the infirmary as soon as possible." He then turned his attention back to Anne, who was breathing slowly but evenly. A tear ran down his cheek as he struggled to understand how an accident like this could have happened. If he had been responsible— even indirectly—for injuring his daughter, he would never be able to forgive himself.

CHAPTER FIVE

Dr. Andrea Kavathis, the physician who ran the lab's small but well-equipped infirmary, leaned over her patient who had finally regained full consciousness. "Well, young lady," she said. "I believe I've got some very good news for you."

Anne looked up eagerly from her hospital bed. It had been more than six hours since she'd been found in the refraction field test chamber and brought to the infirmary. Even so, it was only in the last thirty minutes that she finally started feeling like her old self again.

Sitting beside his daughter, Dr. Felcher clutched Anne's right hand while her mother, who had hurried over to the Johnston & MacNamara complex as soon as she'd gotten word of the accident, tightly held the other.

"Well, are you going to keep us all in suspense?" Anne's father asked expectantly. "Good news is what I want to hear."

Dr. Kavathis brushed aside an unruly lock of her gray-streaked black hair, looked down at the notes on her clipboard, then looked at Anne and smiled. "Your X-rays were very encouraging," she began, "and though you had a concussion, it was very minor. As to the results of all your other tests—the blood panels, the EEG, the EKG—they're all negative."

"Negative?" Anne repeated. "Is that good?"

"It's very good," her father said, smiling warmly. "It means you're fine."

"Well, that's a relief!" her mother said with a sigh. "So when can she go home?"

Anne clutched the ivory cameo in her hand as she waited for the doctor's reply. Her father had returned the necklace to her when she'd regained consciousness. He'd also given her quite a lecture about ruining the experiment, not to mention scaring the living daylights out of him and her mother.

"Mrs. Felcher, Dr. Felcher," Dr. Kavathis said, "Anne needs her rest. Let's continue our discussion outside, shall we?" She motioned toward the door and Anne's parents followed her into the hallway.

"We'll be back in a minute, sweetheart," her dad called over his shoulder as he closed the door behind him.

"Okay, Dad," Anne called back.

But as soon as Dr. Kavathis and her parents were gone, Anne grew suspicious that they might be afraid to talk about her condition in front of her. Curious, she quietly slipped out of bed, padded over to the door, and pressed her ear against it.

"Although Anne shows no signs of any major injuries," Dr. Kavathis was saying, "I'd still like to keep her here for a few more days. No human being has ever been exposed to the kinds of energy fields Anne encountered in that chamber, and I just want to make sure there are no side effects I might have missed."

"What kind of side effects are you talking about Dr. Kavathis?" her mother asked.

"Like I said, I don't exactly know," the physician confessed. There was a moment's pause. "Chances are, your daughter's going to be perfectly fine. But if I'm going to err, I would rather do it on the side of caution."

"I don't think Anne will be too happy about this," her father said. "She's always had tremendous amounts of energy. Being asked to stay in bed all day, especially when she's not feeling sick, will probably drive her nuts."

"We'll do our very best to make her stay as comfortable as possible," Dr. Kavathis promised. "So, shall we go tell her?"

Hearing them walking toward the room, Anne rushed back to the bed and jumped under the covers. A moment later, her parents, followed by

Dr. Kavathis, came into the room. But instead of walking over to her bedside, they stopped in their tracks, looked around curiously, then walked over to the adjacent bathroom.

"Anne?" her mother called.

"What's up?" Anne replied, totally confused by the puzzled look on everyone's faces.

Her father spun around and looked right past her.

"Anne, where are you?" he asked.

"I'm right here, Dad," Anne insisted, waving at him. "Can't you see me?"

"Anne, this isn't funny anymore," Dr. Kavathis said sternly, as she looked in the closet. "Now come out and show yourself."

"What are you all talking about?" Anne demanded, suddenly getting a sick feeling in the pit of her stomach. "I'm right here in this hospital bed. Can't you see me?"

She waved her hand not more than two feet from her father's face. But the man didn't appear to react to it in the slightest.

An expression of pure dread on her face, Anne's mother walked toward the bed, her eyes focused on a spot far beyond where her daughter sat. "Anne, say something," she said with a quaking voice.

"Mom, stop doing this," Anne replied, now looking as frightened as her parents. "I'm right in front of you!"

Now all three adults were cautiously wandering around the room with their hands out in front of them as though they had suddenly gone blind. In turn, Anne reached out to touch each of them. At least she felt like she was reaching out . . . except there was just one big problem—she couldn't see her own arms!

"Mom! Dad!" she cried out. "I'm invisible!" She stared at the place where her arm should have been and saw only the stark white bedsheets below her. Unnerved, she frantically tried to touch her forehead. But because she was now having trouble judging distances, she accidentally bopped herself on the nose. "Ouch!" she yelped.

"Honey, what happened?" her mother asked in alarm. "Are you hurt?"

"No, I'm fine," Anne replied, rubbing her aching nose. But the truth was, she wasn't fine at all. The reason why she had just hit herself with such force was because she had never even seen her own hand coming toward her face!

"Dad? Mom?" she called out, her voice cracking with fear. "I—I'm right here in bed. Are you *sure* you can't see me?"

She lifted the blanket to get out of bed, causing Dr. Kavathis and her parents to gasp in unison. To them, the blanket appeared to rise of its own accord as though part of a magic act.

"Oh, my!" Anne's mother cried in astonishment. "This is impossible!"

Anne's father, his face as white as the hospital sheets, tried to stay calm. "Okay, honey. Now, I want you to grab my hand," he said as he carefully extended his right hand toward the pillow.

Anne tried as best as she could to reach out to her father. But with no visual clues to help her steer her movements, she found herself groping blindly through empty space, like someone trying to find a light switch in a darkened room. Finally, after several unsuccessful attempts, she grabbed hold of her father's fingers and held tight.

"Gotcha!" she declared with relief.

"Good girl," her father said. "Now, I want you to hold still." Keeping a firm grip on Anne with his right hand, he used his left to follow the line of her arm up to her shoulders, then onto her face.

"Yuck!" Anne sputtered as her father's fingers accidentally brushed against her lips.

"Oops, sorry," he quickly apologized, as his hand came to rest on her forehead. "Well, your temperature appears normal. How do you feel?"

"Scared," Anne confessed.

"I understand," he said with a reassuring smile. "But what are you feeling besides that? Are you feeling any physical symptoms? Dizziness? Nausea? Shortness of breath? A tingling in your skin?"

Anne paused and considered each one of the symptoms her father listed. The truth was, except for the fact that she was terrified out of her mind by the prospect of spending the rest of her life as clear as glass, she felt perfectly normal.

"I'm fine," she finally replied. "What's happened to me, Dad? It has to do with the machine in the refraction chamber, doesn't it?"

"That seems to be the logical conclusion," her father replied, stroking his chin in thought.

"Logic-*shmogic!*" her mother cried. "I want my daughter back!"

"So do I, dear," her father said, trying to stay calm. "And don't worry, I intend to—"

"How long will this last?" Anne broke in, tears in her eyes. "Am I going to be like this forever?"

"I don't know," her father admitted, squeezing her hand. "There's no way to tell. But I promise I'm going to do everything possible to make you visible again. Now, just stay right there—and *don't* get out of that bed." He released her hand and went over to talk to Dr. Kavathis, who was still standing by the door, her face a mask of confusion.

"I want a full medical workup on my daughter," Dr. Felcher said urgently.

"But we just did an entire—" Dr. Kavathis began.

"But she wasn't invisible then, was she?" Dr. Felcher shot back. "Look, we've got to find out what's causing this, and if anything can be done to reverse it. Also, I don't want anyone talking about this outside the lab. I'm dead serious. If news of Anne's condition leaks out to the press, it could be—"

He was cut short by Anne's mother, who was still standing by Anne's hospital bed. A moment ago, she'd been staring silently at the seemingly empty sheets. Now that had changed. Now she was screaming.

CHAPTER SIX

"Mom, what's wrong?" Anne cried out.

"Anne—I can see you!" her mother exclaimed joyfully. Flinging her arms wide, she pulled her daughter into a tight embrace.

Instantly, Anne's father rushed over to her bedside, with Dr. Kavathis close behind.

"Dad, can you see me now, too?" Anne asked with tentative excitement.

"Yes, honey!" her father replied, tears of joy in his eyes. He turned to Dr. Kavathis. "You can see her, too, can't you?"

The doctor bobbed her head as tears flowed down her cheeks. "Thank goodness!" she exclaimed with a heavy sigh of relief.

As her mother and father locked her in a big group hug, Anne lifted her hand and was delighted to see that, yes, she could finally see herself again. Then her vision blurred as she began to weep along with everyone else. She was whole again. She was a person, not a freak or an oddity. After having experienced the biggest scare of her entire life, it appeared that her nightmare was over.

At Dr. Kavathis's insistence, Anne remained in the Johnston & MacNamara infirmary for another two days undergoing a new and more thorough set of medical tests. For a full forty-eight hours, Anne was scanned up and down with X-rays, and stuck with more needles than a cactus. But despite Dr. Kavathis's best efforts to find something wrong with her, the tests only proved that Anne was a normal, healthy, and increasingly restless thirteen-year-old girl.

Finally, after reading over all the test results a second time, both Dr. Kavathis and Anne's father agreed that the girl's invisibility had been a freak, temporary phenomenon, one that was unlikely to ever occur again. At long last, they decided it was safe for her to leave the facility and go back to her normal life.

Almost as soon as Anne set foot back in the halls of Thomas Jefferson Junior High, she was treated like a celebrity. Everyone—her teachers included—asked her over and over again about how and why she'd run back to the photon refraction chamber, only to be trapped inside. They also wanted to know the details of her recovery, but most of all, everyone wanted to know what it felt like to be invisible.

Anne, however, as instructed by her father, told everyone that she had no idea how being invisible felt since she'd been unconscious the entire time the invisibility field had been active. She gave no hint that she'd briefly become invisible later on in the infirmary, since her father had specifically told her not to discuss that part of her experience with anyone. This particular aspect of her bizarre adventure, he explained, was still "classified," and bringing the subject up would not do her—or Johnston & MacNamara—any good.

"You mean you don't remember a *thing?*" Judy Slocum probed as she, Anne, and Kara Winowski sat together at lunch that day.

"Nope. Nada. Zippo," Anne assured her.

"Too bad," Kara said, obviously disappointed. "You boldly go where no girl has gone before, and it's like it never even happened!"

The truth was, that's exactly how Anne felt. At this point, the whole horrible incident was feeling more and more like just a bad dream . . . until everything changed later that afternoon.

It happened during her gym class. Anne was in the locker room and she had just changed into her shorts and T-shirt when she went to check herself out in one of the full-length mirrors.

"Oh, great," she mumbled, leaning toward the mirror to examine her skin. "I look so pale. I hope I'm not starting to get sick."

As she ran her fingers over her strangely chalklike skin, Anne suddenly gasped. The image in front of her momentarily blurred. Rubbing her eyes, thinking that she was coming down with a fever, Anne looked again . . . at nothing. Well, not *exactly* nothing. The rest of the locker room behind her was as clear as ever. The only thing that was missing was *her!*

CHAPTER SEVEN

Choking back a scream, Anne spun around to see if anyone had noticed her sudden disappearance. But much to her surprise, all the other girls seemed to be going about their usual business—chatting, putting on their gym clothes, and primping in front of the mirrors. Apparently, everyone was too busy to notice that she had just winked out like a light bulb.

I've got to hide, she thought urgently, immediately realizing how ironic it was that an invisible person was concerned about being seen. Actually, she was concerned about not being seen. That is, she was deathly afraid that someone would run into her and realize that she was, in fact, invisible!

Turning, Anne was about to hurry into the nearby bathroom when exactly what she had feared occurred. One of her classmates, a curly, dark-haired girl named Toni Blanchard, having no idea Anne was standing directly in her path, ran straight into her, painfully knocking them both to the ground.

"Ouch!" Anne cried as she slammed into the tile floor. She turned to see Toni looking confused.

"What happened to you, Toni?" Lisa Connors called from her nearby locker. "Trip over your shoelaces again?"

This joke—as lame as it was—caused Lisa's friends Rita and Hillary to laugh hysterically.

"I—I think I just ran into something," Toni stammered, unaware that the "something" was an invisible eighth grader.

Another girl ran over to help Toni get back on her feet, forcing Anne to quickly roll to one side to avoid being stepped on. Then Anne scrambled to her feet and zigzagged her way through the crowded locker room to the bathroom, being extra careful to avoid colliding with any of the other girls who continued to move by her, totally unaware of her existence.

Once in the bathroom, Anne entered one of the toilet stalls and fumbled with the inside lock. It was still extremely difficult for her to manipulate small objects like this. Her hand–eye coordination was completely off, due to her inability to see her own hands, and so it took Anne several attempts before she managed to grab hold of the sliding metal bolt and secure the door. Grateful for the privacy, she sat down on the toilet seat and sighed with relief.

"What am I going to do now?" she said softly to herself. "Why is this happening to me?"

She held up her right hand—at least, she felt like she was holding it up—and tried to find its shape in the air in front of her. As she did, a strange and wonderful thing happened. For a brief moment, Anne saw the faint outline of her arm briefly shimmer about eighteen inches in front of her nose, then vanish as quickly as it had appeared.

"Did *I* make that happen?" she asked herself. She stared intently at where she figured her hand should be, trying by sheer will to see it. Then, as if by magic, her hand slowly began to materialize.

"Yes!" Anne cried. Then she began to concentrate even harder, determined to bring her entire body back to visibility.

At first, her arm was only a faint shadow, like a ghost image that sometimes appears on television when two signals interfere with each other. But then, as she fixed her attention on the image, Anne happily saw it actually solidify before her eyes. Now, her arm resembled a photographic double exposure. It was clearly visible, but the bathroom door still showed through it.

Clenching her jaw and concentrating so hard that beads of sweat were beginning to form on her temples, Anne struggled to bring her arm completely back to normal. Finally—miraculously—not only one arm solidified, but when Anne raised her other hand, she was delighted to see it, too. The same went for her legs and all the rest of her body. Through sheer force of her own will, Anne Felcher had successfully brought herself back to the visible world!

But she wasn't ready to stop there. *What if I can actually control my invisibility?* Anne thought. *If I can, I could use it like a power—a power I've got to make sure I master completely.*

Excited, Anne now decided to try something different. She raised her hand, fixed her eyes upon it, and thought with all her might, *Disappear!* Then, as she continued to stare at her hand, she imagined with everything she had in her that it was fading away into nothingness. And that's when she saw, to her amazement, her entire arm begin to grow hazy! Within seconds, it became strangely transparent, as if it were made of smoked glass, and then, all at once, it disappeared altogether!

"I've done it!" she cried, triumphantly raising her fist into the air. "I've gotten my invisibility under my control!"

Just then, a pair of legs appeared in front of her and she heard someone pulling at the door.

"Is anyone in there?" a woman asked.

Anne immediately recognized the voice. It was Ms. Atlas, one of the assistant coaches. Should she identify herself? Or should she tell Ms. Atlas that the stall was occupied? Her mind racing, Anne looked down at herself and realized that not only had she made her arm disappear, but her entire body as well. Now, if Ms. Atlas glanced under the closed door, she'd see what appeared to be an empty stall. Deciding she'd better keep her mouth shut, Anne remained perfectly still and silently hoped the coach would just go away.

But Ms. Atlas didn't go away. In fact, just as Anne had feared, she bent down and glanced under the door.

"Darned girls!" she muttered. "I hate it when they do things like this!"

Grumbling angrily, the woman got down on her hands and knees and prepared to crawl under the door. She obviously believed that, as a prank, some girl had locked the door from the inside, then crawled out, leaving the stall inaccessible.

Oh, no! Anne thought, her invisible heart nearly beating out of her invisible chest. There's not enough room in here for both of us!

Needing to act fast, she quickly reached for the lock, then released the bolt and pulled the door inward toward herself.

The surprised look on Ms. Atlas's face was priceless as the door swung open above her, seemingly all by itself. It was all Anne could do to keep from laughing out loud as the gym teacher awkwardly climbed back to her feet, looked curiously at the door, then grabbed hold of it.

Now having to cover her mouth to keep her giggles from escaping, Anne quickly released the door and let Ms. Atlas swing it back and forth as if trying to learn the secret of its unusual behavior. As this happened, Anne pressed herself into the back corner of the stall behind the toilet to keep the door from hitting her on each pass.

"Must have been stuck," Ms. Atlas finally said. Then, apparently satisfied with the solution she'd come up with, she turned and walked out.

Anne pressed her ear to the bathroom door, and only when she heard Ms. Atlas's office door click closed did she allow herself to sigh with relief. "Now," she whispered, "I'd better bring myself back to visibility." She raised her hand to begin staring at it when a sudden inspiration caused her to stop short.

This is too good to waste, she thought, staring into a mirror and seeing absolutely no sign of herself in its reflection. She thought back to the humiliation Lisa Connors had caused her when she slipped that slice of pie onto her chair in the cafeteria. Then she thought about how desperate she'd been to find a way to get back at Lisa without getting caught. Now she had that chance!

Chuckling at the prospects for sweet revenge, Anne turned and headed eagerly for the gym.

CHAPTER EIGHT

When Anne entered the school's cavernous gymnasium, she found two volleyball games just getting underway under the direction of Coach Lloyd, the eighth grade girls' gym teacher. The slap of bouncing balls and the cries of excited players echoed off the gym's cold brick walls as she watched Lisa, Rita, Hillary, and eight other girls battle an equal number of players on the opposite side of the netted court.

"Two to nothing!" Lisa called out from the serving position. She tossed the volleyball high into the air, then smashed it smartly with her fist, sending it sailing smoothly over the net. Toni Blanchard, on the opposing team, caught the incoming ball on her fingertips and set it up nicely for the girl next to her, who then leaped up and smacked it back to Lisa's team.

Hillary Tyler, the team's star player, was already at the net. Leaping into the air, she intercepted the incoming ball with her upraised arm and spiked it back. One of Toni's teammates dived to stop the ball, but she wasn't even close. The ball hit the wooden floor, then bounced away.

Lisa and her teammates cheered.

"Way to go, Hillary!" Lisa shouted above the rest.

"You stink!" Rita shouted tauntingly.

"Come on, let's put those losers out of their misery!" Hillary yelled to her teammates.

"Cut the name-calling, and let's play volleyball!" Coach Lloyd shouted from the other side of the gym.

It looks like it's time to teach Lisa and her friends some humility, Anne thought. Then grinning with sweet anticipation, she crept toward the volleyball players, being extra careful not to let her invisible sneakers squeak on the polished gym floor.

"Three to zippo!" Lisa announced, preparing for her next serve. "We're going for a shutout!"

With that, she tossed the ball into the air. But at the same moment, Anne reached out and grabbed Lisa's right arm just as she pulled it back to smash the ball.

"Whoa!" Lisa exclaimed as she suddenly found her arm firmly locked behind her back. Then Anne released Lisa's arm just in time for the snotty girl to awkwardly smack the ball into the ground.

"Great serve, Lisa!" Toni Blanchard shouted, her voice dripping with sarcasm.

Hillary walked over to Lisa, clearly puzzled. "What happened?" she whispered. "That was the goofiest serve I've ever seen."

"I don't know," Lisa replied, tossing the ball to the opposing team. "It felt like someone grabbed my arm."

"Well, I hope nobody grabs your arm while Toni's serving," Hillary said. "I want to win this game."

As Toni tossed the ball up and gave it a whack, Anne didn't interfere, and it sailed easily over the net. It went back and forth several times, and then Hillary charged the net as she did before in preparation for her spike. But this time, Anne quickly stepped up behind her, and as Hillary jumped, Anne grabbed the back of her shorts and gave them a swift yank.

Missing the ball entirely, Hillary quickly hiked her shorts back up, whirled around, and shouted indignantly, "Hey, who did that?"

Hillary's teammates just stared at her like they didn't have the slightest idea what she was talking about. Which, of course, they didn't.

Feeling more confident than ever, Anne stepped up behind Hillary once again, and this time gave the elastic band on her shorts a good snap!

"Hey, this isn't funny!" Hillary cried, spinning around. But she didn't see another girl within five feet of her. "Whoever's doing this is gonna pay!"

"One-three!" Toni announced as she prepared to take another serve. "Ready?"

Anne made sure Toni didn't lose her serve for the rest of the game. Every time it looked like Lisa's team might get control of the ball, Anne quickly stepped in to invisibly grab a girl's arm, step on her foot, throw an elbow into her ribs, knock the ball out of the air, or otherwise mess up the play. It wasn't long before Lisa and her teammates became so frustrated with their "bad luck" that they began to blame each other for their poor performance, turning their crude insults on themselves instead of the opposing players. As a result of their self-directed anger, they soon were playing poorly even without Anne's help. By the end of the game, Anne could simply stand back and watch Lisa and her friends blow play after play, setup after setup, their poor attitude doing more to lose points than any ghostly girl could ever hope to make them do.

When the period bell rang, Anne—feeling as triumphant as an Olympic gold medal winner—dashed back into the locker room, locked herself in one of the toilet stalls, then concentrated with all her might until she managed to bring herself back to full visibility. Exhausted by the effort, she staggered out of the stall—right into Coach Lloyd.

"Anne!" the woman cried with surprise. "How come I didn't see you in class today?"

You didn't see me because I was invisible, was the answer Anne was tempted to give. But instead she decided to offer a more believable explanation.

"I—uh—wasn't feeling so well, so I went to see the school nurse," Anne replied, immediately realizing as she said this that her lie could be uncovered with a simple call to the nurse's office.

"I hope your not feeling well had nothing to do with what happened at your father's lab," Coach Lloyd said with concern, obviously buying Anne's bogus explanation.

"Uh, no," Anne replied, forcing a smile. "It was just a headache. The nurse just let me lie down for a while. I'm fine now. In fact, I'd better dress and get ready for my next class."

Not wanting to be interrogated one moment longer, Anne bolted straight for her locker. There she grabbed her padlock all ready to dial the combination, only to find it hanging loosely from the hole in the locker handle. Someone had broken her lock!

Her hands suddenly shaking, Anne carefully removed the ruined lock, opened the door, and gasped in shock. Her clothes lay cut up in shreds!

Boy, Lisa, Anne thought, shaking her head. *You've really gone too far this time!* But then she remembered that Lisa and her two nasty friends had been in the gym during the past forty-five

53

minutes. There clearly wasn't enough time before or after class for them to have done this—especially without someone seeing them.

This meant that Anne had a new enemy. An unknown enemy. And the way Anne figured it, she'd better find out who it was before he or she had a chance to strike again.

CHAPTER NINE

"Are you sure you didn't see anyone around here during the class period?" Coach Lloyd asked Ms. Atlas as they both stood in front of Anne's trashed locker.

"Not a soul," Ms. Atlas replied. "My office is right over there. I can safely say that no one—and I mean no one—was in here once the bell sounded."

Anne, standing nearby, wanted to tell the woman that she herself had been in the locker room long after class had started, but decided that bringing up the matter of her invisibility at this time probably wasn't the smartest thing to do. So she just let the teachers work the problem out for themselves.

"Well, then I don't have an answer," Coach Lloyd said, turning to Anne looking somewhat embarrassed. "If you want, we can assign you another locker, and you can use one of my padlocks. That way, whoever did this will have a much harder time doing it again."

"Thanks, Coach," Anne said gratefully. "Now the problem is, what do I wear for the rest of the day?"

Coach Lloyd took Anne to her office where she allowed her to go through the pile of lost-and-found clothing that had accumulated over the years. As Anne waded through the mismatched clothing, trying to find an outfit that looked halfway decent, she kept trying to figure out who might have had an opportunity—not to mention a reason—to break into her locker and ruin her clothes.

But with her three key suspects all having the same perfect alibi, Anne's list was pretty short. For all she knew, the attack might have been totally random. Some sick kid looking to make trouble might have just trashed the first locker in sight. If so, it was probably best for Anne to forget the whole thing and get on with her life.

But Anne couldn't just forget how her favorite sweater was now nothing more than cut-up wool, and so the minute she sat down to lunch with her friends, she blabbed out every detail of the vandalizing incident.

"My mom had something like that happen once to her car," Judy jumped in as soon as Anne finished her story. "She'd left it in the parking lot of the Westside Mall. When she came back an hour later, the lock was busted, the seats were slashed, and everything in the glove compartment had been

56

taken out and thrown around. The weird thing was, whoever broke in didn't steal anything—not even the radio or her cellular phone. And even though the lot was busy, no one saw who did it. It was really creepy."

"Once my brother Carl's dorm room at college got wrecked," Kara said, leaning into the table as if she were revealing government secrets. "It was just like what Judy said happened to her mom's car. They tore the place up, even slashed his mattress, but they didn't steal anything. And he had a real expensive stereo there. They broke it, but they didn't steal it."

"Why would anyone do a thing like that?" Anne asked, suddenly feeling strangely vulnerable. "Why destroy things for no reason?"

"It's a sick world," Kara noted glumly.

Anne nodded, depressed by the realization that, in this world, there were dark forces at work whose logic and purpose she might never understand.

"You want to hear something really sick?" Judy asked, leaning in secretively. "I hear that Harley Stevens asked Sarah Malnotti and Inga Swerlin to the movies with him this Saturday!"

And with that, the conversation veered sharply away from Anne's problems to Harley's gall in trying to get away with asking two girls out on the same night. From there Anne and her friends talked about movies, CDs, and how none of them had a hope of being the movie stars they wanted to be.

One subject that did not come up was Anne's awesome discovery that she could now make herself invisible. Not that Anne wasn't dying to talk about it, but she figured that with Judy and her big mouth at the table, her secret would be all over the North American continent by the end of the week.

In fact, Anne had decided not to tell anyone— not even her parents—about her newfound powers. She knew that, if she did, she'd be back in the Johnston & MacNamara infirmary before she could say "invisible," and that she could easily spend the better part of her teenage years serving as a human guinea pig for any number of scientists eager to learn what made her tick.

Of course, her dad would say he was only looking out for her health—and, of course, he would be—but Anne was old enough to know that there were plenty of other people who would give practically anything to learn how to make humans invisible. In the end, Anne figured she'd be little more than just another laboratory rat, and she was not about to let that happen.

To discipline herself, Anne spent a large part of that afternoon's Spanish class daydreaming about what guidelines she should follow when using her newly developed talent.

I'll only become invisible when it's absolutely necessary, she promised herself. *I'll be extremely careful not to get caught. And I'll only use my powers for good.* She grinned, growing more excited by the second. *I'll be like a superhero! I'll do good deeds all over the city! I'll—*

"That's it, everyone," her teacher, Ms. Gonzales, announced. "Put your pencils down and pass your papers to the front of the class."

Anne looked up from the blank piece of paper on her desk to the vocabulary words on the board. She'd been so distracted by her daydreams of becoming the next Wonder Woman that she hadn't even begun to translate the words written there. As a result, she was going to get the first F of her life.

And then she had an idea. She knew that Ms. Gonzales usually went to the teacher's lounge after this class. The way Anne figured it, all she had to do was quickly translate all the words, turn herself invisible, then sneak into the lounge and slip her paper into the folder! It was, Anne reasoned, not exactly going against the guidelines she'd just devised for herself when using her invisibility. After all, wasn't she using her powers to do good—on a test?

Acting quickly before she changed her mind, Anne copied the twenty Spanish words from the board. Then during her next period, which was study hall, she easily translated the words into English.

Now for the really tricky part, Anne thought as she folded the finished paper, put it into her pocket, then got permission from the study hall monitor to go to the restroom. *Now I've got to become a phantom and get to Ms. Gonzales's folder.*

Once safely out of sight in a bathroom stall, Anne mustered all her strength, focused her concentration, and willed herself to disappear. Soon, just like in gym class, she was completely invisible, and luckily, so was the paper in her shirt pocket.

Now moving unseen down the hall, she quickly made her way to the teacher's lounge. There, as expected, she found Ms. Gonzales sitting at a table correcting the translation quizzes. Creeping up quietly behind the teacher, Anne gently tapped her on the right shoulder.

"What?" Ms. Gonzales asked as she turned around. But much to her surprise, she saw no one there.

Taking her teacher's moment of distraction as her opportunity to carry out the rest of her plan, Anne quickly put her completed paper on top of the others Ms. Gonzales was grading.

Her task complete, Anne stifled a giggle as she watched Ms. Gonzales shrug, then turn back to her work. She picked Anne's paper off the pile and smiled, seeing that one of her best students had once again not disappointed her and had turned in exceptional work.

Cool! Anne thought, happy that she'd pulled off her scheme and avoided a major scholastic disaster. She hung around long enough to see Ms. Gonzales write a big 100 on her paper, then went off to find a bathroom where she could become visible again.

As the day wore on, Anne found herself having the urge to "wink out"—as she now liked to call becoming invisible—more and more. But somehow she managed to stay in control of her powers, at least until after school, when she found herself in a situation that just begged for invisibility.

Tony Gilette—*the* Tony Gilette—was waiting at the school bus stop talking with two of his buddies from the football team, Andy Moss and Patrick Sanford. For a brief moment, Anne stopped and looked his way, and at the very same instant, Tony actually caught her eye—and smiled at her!

The whole thing only lasted a few seconds, but to Anne it felt as if time had suddenly stood still. Tony was, after all, the most desirable boy in the entire eighth grade. He was not only good looking, but he was smart, athletic, and had a brother who drove a sports car. Tony could even be downright charming—when he wanted to be—which is a lot more than she could say for most of the other boys in her class. The very idea that he would even look her way, let alone smile at her, was enough to make Anne's head do a quick three-sixty.

Returning to "real time," Anne now saw that Tony had turned away and once again was talking with his friends. But it was too late for Anne. He'd already hooked her heart. Maybe he's talking about me! she thought excitedly. And then she realized that she could actually find out.

Throwing her guidelines for invisibility out the window, Anne began scanning the area for a place to hide so she could "wink out." Noticing a large concrete retaining wall by the nearby steps, she walked over, peered behind it, and saw that it provided excellent cover. Then, checking about to make sure she wasn't being watched, she ducked behind the wall, set down her backpack, lifted her hand in front of her face, and began to concentrate. Slowly, from her fingers to her toes, Anne Felcher faded from sight.

Leaving her backpack on the ground, the now invisible Anne dashed out from behind the retaining wall and hurried over to where Tony was still talking with his friends. Careful to avoid bumping into any of the boys, she leaned in closely and began to eavesdrop on their conversation.

"No way Chicago's gonna make a trade like that with St. Louis," Andy Moss was saying.

"The whole story was on the news this morning," Patrick Sanford insisted. "The deal went down for at least ten million dollars."

"That was just the *offer*, you moron," Tony said, exasperated. "No one's signed anything yet. They're talking about it."

"Who are you calling a moron, you chowderhead?" Patrick challenged.

"And just who are you calling a chowderhead, lamebrain?" Tony shot back.

Unseen by any of them, Anne slowly walked away. *I should have known,* she thought, completely dejected. *There's no way a group of boys is going to talk about me over sports.*

Feeling like she was completely wasting her special powers, Anne was about to go retrieve her backpack when something caught her eye. At first, it looked to her as if a strange animal was sitting atop the nearby retaining wall. But as she got closer, Anne saw that it wasn't an animal at all—at least no animal she'd ever seen before.

About the size of a large monkey, the creature had a short, stocky body covered with greenish-gray fur. Its oversized head sported two big, shiny eyes like huge black marbles, and its face had a weird, reptilian look, kind of like that of an angry monster. To Anne, the creature looked like one of the hideous gargoyles that adorned the roof of the old cathedral in the center of town.

What is that horrible thing? she wanted to shout, then quickly remembered she was invisible.

But almost as if it had heard her shout anyway, the creature suddenly turned Anne's way and locked its huge black eyes with her green ones. Then, moving with catlike speed, it leaped up on its short but powerful legs and raised its crooked arms to reveal a pair of talonlike claws.

It's alive! Anne realized in terror.

A moment later, the living gargoyle lifted its huge, ugly head and gave a piercing shriek like the cry of an eagle. Then, unfolding a pair of broad, leathery wings, it leaped into the air and came flying straight at Anne!

CHAPTER TEN

Anne screamed and threw herself to the ground just as the hideous monster streaked overhead. She hit the concrete with a painful thump, and cried aloud as she scraped her palms on the rough pavement. For several seconds she lay there cowering, shielding her head with her hands as she waited for the creature to slash into her with its knifelike claws. But nothing happened.

"Are you all right?" she heard someone say.

Realizing that she must have somehow snapped back to visibility, Anne uncovered her head to see Tony Gilette standing over her, his face filled with concern. "What happened?" he asked.

Anne's eyes darted about nervously as she slowly sat up and scanned the skies for any sign of the frightful gargoyle. But all she saw were the stunned faces of her fellow classmates, all of whom were looking at her as if she were out of her mind.

"Did you see it?" Anne asked fearfully.

"See what?" Tony asked. He clearly had no idea what Anne was talking about.

How is that possible? Anne wondered. *How could anyone have missed that awful thing? Unless . . . it was invisible, too!* Then another scary thought occurred to her. *What if someone saw me materialize?*

"Did you trip or something?" Tony was asking.

Anne heaved a secret sigh of relief. Apparently everyone had been far too busy getting away from school to notice a girl suddenly appearing amongst them out of thin air.

"Uh, yeah, I guess I tripped," Anne said. Then she slowly got back to her feet.

"Here," said Tony, offering his hand like a knight in shining armor. "Let me help you up."

"Thanks," Anne said, realizing that she was shivering, not because it was cold, but because Tony still held her hand. "I—uh—guess I should be going," she said, casting her eyes away shyly as Tony let her go with a warm smile.

"Uh, where are your books?" he asked, looking around the empty sidewalk. "Don't you usually carry a brown backpack?"

"Y-yes," Anne replied, amazed that Tony had even noticed her enough to know she *owned* a backpack.

She hurried over to the retaining wall, surprised to find that Tony was following close behind her.

"It's Anna, isn't it?" he asked, his voice unsteady.

CHAPTER TEN

"Anne," she replied, grabbing her backpack by its strap. "With an 'e' on the end."

"Why was your pack back here?" Tony asked.

For a moment, Anne hesitated, unsure of how to respond. What was she supposed to tell him? That she needed to ditch her pack here while she turned invisible and went to eavesdrop on him and his friends? No, it was better to do what her parents always did when she raised an uncomfortable issue—change the subject.

"Some weather we're having, huh?" she blurted out as she hurried toward her waiting bus.

"Yeah, it's been really—uh—*normal*," Tony replied awkwardly as he fell in stride next to her. Then, as Anne boarded the bus, he called to her, "Well, I guess I'll see you around, huh?"

"Right," Anne replied, pausing at the doorway and flashing him a smile. "See you!"

Aboard the bus, Anne sat alone scolding herself for being such a nerd in front of Tony. *Some weather we're having?* She couldn't believe how lame she was. It had been her first chance to have a conversation with the school hunk, and all she did was talk about the weather. Pathetic!

All the way home, Anne replayed the entire scene, inventing all sorts of wonderfully witty remarks she could have said to impress Tony. But she knew it was a pointless exercise. She'd blown a golden opportunity—in fact, she'd made a total fool of herself in front of the unquestionably coolest boy in the whole school. Now all she wanted to do was disappear. To never show her face again. Of course, the truth was, she actually could do this now. She could make sure that she never had to face Tony Gilette or Lisa Connors or anyone else ever again. In fact, she could make it so no one could find her for the rest of her life.

But as tempting as that seemed at the moment, the more Anne considered it, the less attractive permanent invisibility looked to her. After all, there were worse things than embarrassing yourself in front of someone as incredible as Tony Gilette—like being ignored. And if she made herself disappear, that's exactly what would happen to her. People would look right through her— literally. She could be in a room with a hundred other people, and no one would give her so much as a glance. That would be truly frightening. If that happened, she might as well be dead.

Anne was just about to go back to worrying about facing Tony again when she remembered something else that had just rocked her world. Less than an hour ago she'd been attacked by a flying creature straight out of a medieval nightmare. All her life, grown-ups had told her that such monsters didn't exist, and yet here was actual evidence that they did.

But how could she prove their existence? The monster had been invisible to everyone but her . . . and she had only seen it when she was invisible as well. Did this mean that there were other creatures, both monster and human, in the invisible world? The very idea sent a chill up Anne's back.

Hurrying up the sidewalk, she found herself glancing nervously at trees and rooftops, wondering if, even now, gargoyles like the one she'd seen at school were perched up there watching her and plotting their next assault.

Finally, just as she reached the foot of her driveway, Anne decided she had to know the truth, no matter how awful it might be. Moving behind the trunk of the large oak tree that stood in her front lawn, she set down her backpack, checked to see that no one was around, then concentrated on disappearing.

Nervous about what she might see, Anne, now fully transparent, stepped out from behind the tree and again looked around at the surrounding rooftops.

"Are you up there?" she shouted. "If you are, show yourselves! I'm not afraid of you!"

She continued to look about, but nothing seemed out of the ordinary.

Maybe I just imagined it, she thought hopefully.

Relieved, Anne turned to go hide and make herself visible again when she suddenly found herself face to face with the most hideous monster she'd ever seen. It was squatting on the roadside mailbox directly in front of her and, just like the creature she had seen at school, it was covered with shaggy, greenish-gray fur. But unlike the first gargoyle, this one had the face of a disgusting insect, complete with bulging red eyes and a clawlike jaw. Giving a high-pitched laugh, it snapped its forked tongue straight at her, then leaped into the air with its thick muscular legs.

Anne screamed and turned to run away, and as she did, she felt the creature land squarely on her back, hooking its right arm around her throat. Nearly crazed with fear, Anne batted her arms and spun wildly about in the middle of the street, trying to shake loose the awful monster.

"Get off of me!" she shouted. "Help, somebody! Please, help me!"

Now, in addition to the creature's high-pitched laugh, she heard another sound. It was the roar of a gasoline engine. And it was quickly getting louder. Alarmed, Anne spun about and her eyes grew wide with terror. A motorcycle was heading straight for her! And because she was invisible, the driver had no idea she was standing directly in his path!

CHAPTER ELEVEN

Just as the motorcycle was about to crash into Anne head-on, the gargoyle on her back shrieked and hurled itself directly at the oncoming cyclist. Although he had no way of seeing the invisible creature as it flew toward him, the cyclist reacted as anybody would if something about the size of a chimpanzee landed directly on his head. His hands flew up toward his face, and he completely lost control of his motorcycle.

As Anne dived to the right, the runaway bike skidded by on her left, missing her by such a narrow margin that she could feel the heat from its chrome exhaust pipes. Still traveling at probably thirty miles per hour, the cycle finally fell onto its side and slid across the pavement until it came to rest against the concrete curb several yards away.

This was the second time in as many hours that Anne had fallen onto paved earth, and just like at school, when she sat up, she discovered that her body had spontaneously returned to a visible state. It seemed that the physical shock of such a fall was enough to break her concentration and force her to revert back to her natural physical condition.

As for the motorcyclist, he was lying on the street nearby, stunned but apparently unharmed.

"Are you okay, mister?" Anne called, running up to the young man who was now sitting up and stiffly removing the scarred helmet from his head. "You want me to call an ambulance?"

"No, I'm okay," he grunted, shaking out his sweaty, long blond hair. "No broken bones. Just a few bruises, that's all." With Anne's help, he pulled himself to his feet, then brushed the dirt off his leather pants. "Must have hit a pothole or something." He looked about, and was visibly surprised to see that the area where he'd fallen was smoothly paved. "Hmmm, that's strange."

Anne was tempted to explain that he'd been knocked over by an invisible flying gargoyle just so she could see his reaction, but she wisely decided to let the cyclist come to his own conclusions, as wrong as they might be.

"Need help with your bike?" she offered, walking over to the motorcycle now lying by the curb.

"No, thanks, I've got it," he said. He walked over and lifted the heavy machine upright. Then he slipped his helmet back on, tightened the chin strap, mounted the bike, and tried to kick-start the engine. It took three tries, but the motor finally caught, and giving a shaky wave, the motorcyclist roared away blissfully unaware that he'd just survived a close encounter with the terminally weird.

Back in her bedroom, Anne began to mentally assemble the pieces to the puzzle that her life had become. It was now painfully clear to her that the universe, as most people understood it, was only part of a much greater picture. Just as the human eye could only see a small portion of the light spectrum, people were equally blind to that part of reality where monsters dwelled. Here, in a dimension that existed parallel to her own, Anne now realized that monsters right out of ancient myths and fairy tales were wreaking all kinds of havoc on whomever and whatever they pleased.

Call them what you wanted—gargoyles, gremlins, imps, or bogeymen—they were real creatures that could not only see people, but were able to physically interact with them when they chose to. The way Anne figured it, these mischievous, unseen monstrosities could easily be the cause of the recent disturbances right here in her own house, the trashing of her gym locker at school, and even the strange occurrences Judy and Kara had talked about at lunch.

Anne also realized that although the monsters could see her all the time, she could only see them when she became invisible and entered their realm. At that point, something about her other-worldly state made the creatures suddenly pay special attention to her. It was as if, by becoming invisible to people, Anne became supervisible to the gargoyles. This is why they attacked her. They didn't like her invading their private territory. In fact, their behavior suggested that they actually considered her to be a threat.

I've got to tell Dad about this, she thought, dismissing her earlier decision not to reveal her newfound powers to anyone. *Maybe he can think of a way for me to fight these monsters.*

And so that night, as the Felcher family sat down to dinner, Anne debated how to raise this strange and alarming subject without upsetting her parents and causing them to immediately ship her back to the Johnston & MacNamara Laboratories. As it turned out, anxiety must have been reflected in her face, because both her parents immediately started to question her.

"Is something bothering you, sweetheart?" her father asked as he poured dressing over his salad.

"You do look a little peculiar, Anne," her mother said. "Did things go okay at school today?"

"Well, someone broke into my gym locker," Anne replied, sounding like this sort of thing happened every day, "and they kind of destroyed my clothes." She pointed to the mismatched outfit she still wore. "Coach Lloyd let me borrow this stuff from the lost and found."

"Your locker was vandalized?" her mother gasped.

"Do they know who did it?" her father asked.

"Or why they picked you?" her mother added, still obviously upset.

"Actually, no," Anne responded, wanting to say that catching the culprits was unlikely, seeing as how they were probably invisible gargoyles. Instead, she decided to get right to the point. "Uh, Mom, Dad," she began nervously. "There's something I have to tell you."

Her mother and father set down their knives and forks and turned to Anne expectantly.

"Remember what happened back at the lab?" she asked, her voice shaking. "Remember when I became invisible for a few minutes?"

"How could we forget?" her mother replied with a tense laugh. "We thought we'd lost you forever."

"Well, it happened again," Anne said. "In fact, it turns out that I can actually make myself invisible whenever I want."

Half expecting her parents to scream, or laugh, or cry—but at least expecting some kind of a reaction—Anne sat there dumbfounded as she watched her mother and father silently staring at her. Then, figuring she had nothing to lose, she smiled weakly and added, "Uh, there's more."

"More?" her mother asked, looking like she was about to faint dead away at any moment.

Beginning with her rigging of the volleyball game, going through her first encounter with the gargoyle outside of school, and ending with the appearance of the second monster on the mailbox right outside their home, Anne carefully recounted each of the day's strange events. Her parents listened with rapt attention, and probably would have called the nearest mental hospital if they'd been like most other parents. But, of course, Dr. and Mrs. Felcher were not like other parents. They'd actually "seen" their daughter become invisible. And if that could happen, why couldn't nightmarish creatures also exist in this invisible world?

"I think these monsters know I can see them," Anne went on, suddenly unable to keep her lower lip from trembling. "Mom . . . Dad . . . I'm really scared. What do you think I should do?"

Anne's parents exchanged a quick, silent glance, then her mother got up and gave Anne a warm hug. "Everything's going to be okay, sweetheart," she said, sounding like she was trying to convince herself as well.

"Can you become invisible any time you want?" her father asked, not even bothering to hide his scientific curiosity. "I mean, do you have this, uh, power totally under your control?"

"Uh-huh," Anne responded, bobbing her head up and down.

"Like, right now?" he went on.

"Should I show you?" Anne asked.

"Please," he replied.

After her mother had gone back to her seat, Anne prepared to "wink out." She took a deep breath and relaxed her body. Then noticing her reflection in her water glass, she decided to use it to monitor her progress. She locked her gaze on the distorted image, focused all her energies on the glass, and willed herself to vanish. To her amazement—for this was the first time she'd ever actually watched herself disappear—Anne saw her own reflection quickly fade away to nothingness.

"My goodness!" her mother gasped, putting her hand to her mouth.

"Anne, are you still there?" her father asked urgently, rising from his chair.

"Yup," Anne assured him.

"Take my hand," he said, reaching out.

Anne did as she was told.

"Incredible," her father muttered. "Now, can you bring yourself back?"

"Of course," Anne said confidently. She was just about to "wink back" when she happened to catch signs of movement out of the corner of her eye. Turning to her right, she was stunned to see not one, but three hideous-looking gargoyles sitting atop the nearby china cabinet!

CHAPTER TWELVE

"Oh, no!" Anne yelped, quickly pulling away from her father.

"Anne, what is it?" her mother demanded as she leaped to her feet in alarm.

"The gargoyles!" Anne cried. "Watch out! There're three of them!"

"Where?" her father shouted, searching around blindly. "Where are the gargoyles?"

"Right there!" Anne yelled, pointing to the trio of monsters across the room. Then she realized that her parents couldn't see her pointing and added, "They're on the china cabinet!"

"I can't see anything!" her mother insisted, tears of frustration welling up in her eyes.

Just then, each of the gargoyles snarled, spread their batlike wings, and launched themselves toward Anne.

"Ahhh!" she screamed, diving for cover under the dining room table. But before she'd gotten safely underneath, Anne felt one of the monster's hawkish talons brush by her hair. Then, as she cowered in fear, she heard the flapping of wings as all three of the hideous creatures spun around for yet another attack.

"Anne, you've got to tell us what's going on," her father demanded.

"They're attacking me!" Anne shrieked. "Help!"

"How can we help you?" her mother screamed. "We have no idea where you are!"

Panicked, both of Anne's parents began waving their arms through the air as if trying to make contact with their daughter's invisible assailants.

"We've got to be careful!" her father warned. "We don't want to hit Anne!"

But unbeknownst to Anne's parents, the invisible gargoyles were watching them, and apparently getting a real kick out of seeing the humans vainly trying to attack what they could not see. Then one creature, who narrowly escaped a solid right hook from Anne's father, grinned evilly with its lipless mouth, dove straight for the frustrated scientist, and dug its sharp claws into his forearm.

"Ouch!" Anne's father screamed as his shirt ripped at the sleeve and white hot pain shot through his arm. Unable to believe anything that was happening, he just stared in awe as blood began to well up through a deep gash in his skin.

Seeing that her father had been hurt, Anne leapt to her feet and grabbed a fork from the table—which, to her parents, seemed to rise into the air all by itself. Then, with all three winged monsters circling above her, she jabbed at the air in a vain attempt to wound one of the horrible creatures.

"Go away!" she snarled, more angry than afraid. "Get out of this house! Leave us alone!"

"Anne, come back to us right now!" her father ordered, now holding a cloth napkin over his bleeding wound. "Make yourself visible this instant!"

Responding to her father's command, Anne froze in place and struggled to focus her mind on returning her body to its natural state. But before she could accomplish this, two of the gargoyles started to dive straight for her head. Raising her arms to protect herself, she turned and did the only thing she could do—run!

"Your father's right!" her mother shouted. "Become visible and these things will leave you alone!"

But by this time Anne was already out of the dining room. Her head down, her arms batting the air around her, she stumbled into the kitchen in search of some kind of a weapon. Throwing open a counter drawer, she grabbed the first large item she could lay her hands on.

"Take that!" Anne growled, viciously swinging a heavy wooden rolling pin through the air like a bat.

Then she caught one of the incoming beasties across the side of its body with a loud *thwack!* and sent it crashing to the ground.

But Anne didn't have time to celebrate her small victory. The other two creatures, clearly angered by her successful attack on their repulsive pal, now launched a massive counteroffensive attack. One landed on the stove, picked up the blender off the nearby countertop, shrieked, and hurled it toward Anne. Seeing it coming, she quickly prepared to bat it away with her rolling pin, but before she could, the blender's electrical cord snapped taut, and the glass pitcher shattered against the far wall while the plastic base swung back and slammed into the counter doors.

At practically the same moment, the second beast grabbed a dirty frying pan out of the water-filled sink and flung it skyward. Anne ducked as the heavy iron skillet sailed over her head, then smashed into the refrigerator with a resounding clang!

Running to the kitchen doorway, Anne's parents just stood there, their mouths agape as they watched their kitchen being torn apart by what appeared to be a legion of ghosts. Spoons, knives, and forks flew from an open drawer and went spinning out in all directions. Pots and pans sailed through the air, seemingly of their own accord. Then the refrigerator door flew open and food began flying everywhere as if it were being shot from an invisible cannon. A large jelly jar appeared to leap out of the refrigerator, fly across the counter, then hurl itself to the floor where it shattered into a hundred pieces. And all the while, a rolling pin whipped back and forth as if being swung by the ghost of some deceased baseball player.

"Anne?" her mother called. "Are you all right?"

But Anne was too busy to even formulate an answer. Realizing that the gargoyles were gaining the upper hand, she flung the rolling pin at one of the monsters, then bolted from the room through the doorway opposite from where her parents were standing.

Running as fast as she could, she vaulted up the stairs, made a sharp turn at the second floor landing, and ran straight into her bedroom. Once inside, she slammed the door and threw her body against it.

"Safe at last," she said, gasping for breath. Then, as her lungs fought for air, she tried to listen for any sounds of the monsters outside her door. Not hearing the beating of their awful wings, the cries of their hoarse, high-pitched screeches, or the scratching of their deadly claws on the hallway's hardwood floors, she let out a huge sigh of relief. She'd beaten them . . . or so she thought.

Turning back to her room, she noticed her self-portrait sitting on the easel where she'd left it several days before. But now there was something odd about the painting. Something very odd. And then Anne realized it was the portrait's eyes. When she'd last worked on the piece, she was in the middle of finishing them, only now they appeared to be complete. But instead of being green like her own, these eyes were black and shiny . . . and they were blinking!

The next moment, the portrait exploded outward as a powerful claw punched its way through from the back, revealing the biggest and ugliest gargoyle Anne had yet seen.

Cackling, the monster glared at Anne through the tattered canvas, then smiled in murderous glee.

"Ahhhhhhh!" Anne screamed so loudly that the monster itself jerked back and shrieked as well. Then, not wasting another second, Anne tore open her door and bolted into the bathroom down the hall, slamming the door behind her. After making a quick check of the vanity, under the sink and behind the shower curtain, Anne was finally satisfied that she was safe, so she punched in the lock in the doorknob and sank to the cold tile floor in complete exhaustion. Now all she had to do was gather the energy to become visible again, and this nightmare— at least for the time being—would be over.

Struggling to stay calm, Anne positioned herself in front of the bathroom mirror where, as expected, she saw nothing but the wall behind her. She took a deep breath, flexed her fingers, then stared at the point where she expected her reflection to appear.

"Concentrate," she told herself, shutting her eyes—or at least it felt like she shut her eyes. Since she was invisible, Anne's eyelids were also transparent, which meant she could see right through them. She shuddered to think what would happen if she tried to sleep like this. Shaking off the bizarre thought, Anne tried to refocus. "Now, think!" she commanded herself. "Think about becoming visible again."

She tried to imagine herself becoming visible. She thought about her green eyes, her shoulder-length blond hair, even the lost-and-found shirt she was currently wearing. But this time, no matter how hard Anne tried, no matter how much effort she used, she couldn't seem to materialize. In fact, there wasn't even a glimmer of an outline around where she stood. No distortion of light. No shimmer of color. Nothing.

"Anne?" she heard her father call from the other side of the locked door. "What's happening? Are you all right?"

Anne didn't reply. Instead, she again focused all her attention on the mirror, gritted her teeth, and tried to physically force herself back to visibility.

Come on! she thought, straining every single muscle in her body. *You did this before without even breaking a sweat!* But for a second time, she met with utter failure.

"Anne, we know you're in there. Now open the door!" her mother insisted. "Please, Anne, talk to us!"

Anne now felt, but couldn't see, tears welling up in her eyes. Something was terribly, terribly wrong. All the previous times she had "winked out," she had been able to snap back, sometimes without even trying. But now, for some unexplained reason, she appeared to be totally powerless.

What if I can't become visible again? she thought with rising terror. Now tears were trickling down her cheeks and she had to get a tissue to blow her nose. *How can I possibly spend the rest of my life like this? I'll be in a room and no one will know I'm there. I'll talk to people and they won't even be able to look at me. It'll be like I'm a ghost. A lonely living ghost!*

CHAPTER THIRTEEN

"Anne!" her parents called in unison when they heard their daughter sniffling. "Open this door!"

"Okay, okay," Anne called, unlocking the door. Then, upon seeing her distraught parents standing there in the hallway, she unleashed a flood of tears.

"Sweetheart," her mother said, worry in her voice as she searched the bathroom for any sign of her daughter. "Did those creatures hurt you?"

"Are they still here?" her father asked, looking about the bathroom nervously.

"No to both," Anne replied. "The monsters aren't here, but, as you can tell, neither am I." Once again, she burst into hysterical tears. "I—I've been trying to come back, but I can't. I think I'm stuck!"

"Do you think this has anything to do with those invisible monsters?" her mother asked. "Do you think they're doing this to you?"

"I don't know. I don't think so," Anne replied. In truth, she hadn't even considered the possibility that the gargoyles could in any way interfere with her ability to wink in or out.

Anne's father rubbed his chin, thinking. Then he looked gravely at his wife. "The only thing to do is take Anne back to the laboratory," he said decisively. "I'll put my entire staff on her case." Then he turned to where he thought Anne might be. "First we're going to figure out what happened to you, sweetheart. And then we'll figure out how to reverse it."

"No!" Anne cried fearfully. "I'm not going back to Johnston & MacNamara! I'm not going to be treated like some kind of lab animal."

"Oh, Anne, I'd never let them do that to you!" her father insisted.

"Listen to your father," her mother pleaded. "He only wants to help you."

"I know you're scared, sweetheart," her father said sympathetically. "But it's not safe for you to be at home. Those monsters may be gone for now, but I'm betting they're going to come back. You've got to be where there are people who can help you."

Anne had to admit her father had a point. Those awful creatures were probably hovering somewhere around the house, waiting to pounce on her as soon as she let down her guard. It only made sense for her to go to a secured building, and the labs at Johnston & MacNamara were probably as secure as Fort Knox. Of course, there were no guarantees that the monsters couldn't sneak into the lab, too. After all, even the most advanced security systems in the world were probably useless against invisible flying gremlins. Still, common sense told Anne that she'd be far better off at the lab than here at her house.

"All right, Dad, I'll go," she said with resignation.

"Good. We should leave immediately," he replied. "I'll drive you there right now."

"That's an excellent idea," Anne's mother agreed. "I'll pack up some things and meet you there later."

"Can you find your way to the car, Anne?" her father asked, motioning toward the stairs.

"Of course I can!" she replied indignantly. "Just because I'm invisible doesn't mean I can't see!"

Before heading downstairs, Anne paused to take one last look back at her bedroom. The huge gargoyle that had been in there earlier was gone, but the tattered remnants of her half-completed self-portrait remained. Staring at the picture lying in shreds, she couldn't help but wonder if she'd ever see that face—*her* face—ever again.

Anne and her father arrived at the gates of the Johnston & MacNamara Laboratories just before eight o'clock that evening. When her dad pulled up to the security booth, she half expected the guard to ask him why his daughter was with him at such an unusual hour, but the man didn't even acknowledge Anne's presence and simply wished her father a good evening and waved the car through. It wasn't until they were rolling into the lab's parking structure that Anne realized the man hadn't even seen her sitting in the front seat. As far as the guard knew, her father was alone.

Anne encountered similar treatment when they checked in with the individual who manned the administration building's front desk. An ex-police officer in his late fifties, the man greeted her father with a warm smile and even called him by name. He then buzzed them both into the main lab, unaware that he was buzzing in two people instead of just one.

The government really should be interested in me, Anne thought as she walked undetected behind her father into the lab infirmary. Being invisible, I could get into any building in the world. I'd make the perfect spy!

But Anne decided not to express these thoughts aloud, even to her father, since becoming America's youngest undercover agent was the last thing she wanted to do right now. At present, she had only one objective—to find her way back to the visible world.

Anne and her father were met in a private examination room by Dr. Kavathis. "I came over as soon as I got your call," she said, referring to the urgent message Anne's father had left from his car phone as soon as they'd left the house. "Is Anne with you?"

"I'm right here," Anne said, tapping the doctor on the shoulder.

Dr. Kavathis nearly jumped out of her shoes, then quickly tried to cover up her embarrassment. "Well, then," she said, in the most professional tone she could muster as she turned to Dr. Felcher, "when would you like to get started?"

"Immediately," he replied. "I don't want Anne to be like this a second longer than she has to."

"All right," Dr. Kavathis agreed. She turned to where she believed Anne was standing, although her aim was actually about three feet off. "Here you go, Anne," she said, holding out a laboratory gown she retrieved from a drawer. "Put this on so we'll know where you are."

Anne took the light blue cotton hospital smock and slipped it on over her shoulders. But as soon as she did, the garment vanished from sight.

"How did you do that?" Dr. Kavathis asked with genuine curiosity.

Anne shrugged. "I don't know," she confessed. "When I'm invisible, anything that's against or close to my body becomes invisible, too. It's like there's this narrow invisibility field that's all around me."

"But it appears that when she's merely holding an object and most of that object isn't in contact with her body—" Anne's father jumped in, then smiled for Anne's benefit. "—say like when she's wielding a rolling pin, that object will not disappear. It probably all has something to do with the difference between people and inanimate objects, too," he went on, "since whenever I've grabbed Anne's hand or even hugged her, I remain totally visible."

"Well, Dr. Felcher," Dr. Kavathis said with an amused look on her face, "all this is certainly going to make things, shall we say, interesting for my staff and me when we try to examine your daughter. No one here has been trained to treat patients they can't see!"

For the next few days, Anne Felcher didn't show up at Thomas Jefferson Junior High—or anywhere else, for that matter. While her teachers and classmates were under the impression that she was home sick with a bad flu, Anne was really at the Johnston & MacNamara Laboratories undergoing just about every medical test known to science.

Of all the tests the doctors performed, the worst, as far as Anne was concerned, involved drawing blood. She'd always hated the very idea of having a needle stuck into her arm, but at least in the past she'd been visible, and the nurses could see where to stick their hypodermics. Now that her arms and veins were transparent, the medical staff had to operate using only their sense of touch, feeling for the veins and hoping they got their needles in the right spots. Usually they had to stick her several times before they got it right, and Anne was sure that if she was visible, her arm would be black and blue.

But as painful as drawing blood was, and as uncomfortable as nearly all the other tests were, Anne put up with them, hoping that in the end they would bring her back to the visible world and far away from those horrible gargoyle creatures.

So far, ever since the invisible monsters had torn apart her house, Anne had not seen any sign of them. But she knew all too well that they might return. In fact, even as the research team went about poking, prodding, and measuring her with even more instruments than they'd used the first time she was there, Anne kept her eyes peeled for any signs of greenish-gray fur and listened for the beating of approaching wings.

In the meantime, while Anne was being studied by Dr. Kavathis and her medical staff, Dr. Felcher returned to the photon refraction chamber where he repeatedly tried to duplicate the conditions under which his daughter had gained her powers of invisibility in the first place. Working feverishly, he and his team of scientists placed several different lab animals in the chamber, ranging from white mice to rabbits, exposed them to the chamber's invisibility field, then waited to see if any of them would spontaneously disappear later. But none of them did.

Undaunted, the scientists continued to repeat the experiment using different animals and a variety of field strengths in various combinations. It was their hope that if they could eventually develop an understanding of the forces that had trapped Anne in her nightmare world, they could safely get her out.

Finally, on the fourth day of what Anne called her "invisible imprisonment," her father walked into her hospital room and told both Anne and her mother he'd "found something very interesting."

"Take a look at this," he said, holding up a vial of dark red fluid for them to see.

"Is that my blood?" Anne asked.

"It sure is," her father reported. "It was drawn from you earlier today."

"Don't remind me," Anne said with a groan, the pain of the needles still fresh in her mind . . . not to mention her arm.

"Look at it," her father said, holding the test tube closer to where he imagined Anne's eyes to be. "What do you see?"

"I see blood," Anne replied, stating the obvious.

"Exactly," her father said, smiling. "This is your blood, yet it's perfectly visible. I can see it. We all can see it."

"So what does that mean?" Anne's mother asked. She looked exhausted from having slept on a cot in her daughter's room for two of the four nights Anne had been there.

"Well, we're not sure exactly. But it suggests that Anne's problem doesn't exist at the molecular level." The gifted scientist and worried father rubbed his eyes. He'd been working around the clock to solve the mystery of his daughter's invisibility. "If Anne's blood was naturally invisible, it should stay invisible even after being taken out of her body. But since it doesn't—and since any clothing Anne wears also disappears once it comes in contact with her skin— it suggests that her body is generating some type of light refraction field that affects only those things directly around it."

"You want to say that in plain English?" Anne asked, now totally confused.

"Hmmmm, how can I put this?" her father said thoughtfully. He paced a few moments, then turned back to face where he thought his daughter was. "Try to think of yourself as a stove."

"Fine, I'm a stove," Anne said, playing along. "Gas or electric?"

"Electric," he answered with a warm smile. "Now, when you put a pan on a burner, the pan gets hot, right? But when you take the pan off the stove, it eventually cools back down."

"So I'm like a burner," Anne said, beginning to understand the concept. "But instead of making things hot when I touch them, I make them invisible. Right?"

"Exactly," her father concurred. "Only somehow your controls got stuck in the 'on' position."

"So what do we do?" Anne asked. "Call someone who fixes appliances?"

"No," her dad said. "We pull your plug."

"We what?" her mother exclaimed.

"I didn't mean it that way," Anne's father quickly corrected himself. "I meant that this invisibility field must be getting its power from somewhere. If we can cut that power source—pull the plug, if you will— then we should be able to get Anne back to normal."

At that moment, Anne's father's pocket telephone beeped and he flipped it open. "Felcher," he answered curtly into the mouthpiece. He listened for a moment, then said, "I'll be right there." With that, he flipped the phone closed. "I'm needed in the control room," he said to Anne's mother. Then he held out his hand for Anne who reached over and squeezed it. "You'll be all right, sweetheart," he told her, determination in his eyes.

"I know I will, Dad—with you on the case," Anne replied, wishing he could see her smile.

While Anne's father was gone, her mother left to do a few errands. "Get some rest, honey," she said, closing the door.

For a moment, Anne just lay there listening to her mother's retreating steps on the infirmary's polished linoleum floors. Then she picked up her book and started to read. But after having had her sleep repeatedly disturbed while nurses checked on her day and night, Anne soon grew sleepy, so she put the book aside and turned off the light. Soon her limbs grew limp and her breathing became shallow and regular. She was just about to fall into a deep sleep, when, out of nowhere, she heard something move in the darkness. Instantly Anne's heart began to flutter and her stomach tightened. Had one of those horrid creatures found her?

Without moving a muscle, Anne focused her attention on the room around her, listening for another disturbance. And then she heard the distinct flutter of wings. Her heart going a million miles an hour, Anne then heard an odd, high-pitched chirping, like the sound of a chipmunk. But what was in her room was no palm-sized forest creature, Anne was sure of that.

Ever so cautiously, she moved her hand toward the electrical cord hanging by the side of her bed.

Finding the thick wire, she felt along its length until she came to the plastic switch. Then, sucking in her breath, she snapped it toward her, instantly bathing the room with fluorescent light.

But there wasn't much Anne could see. Something was blocking her face. It was another face. It was the face of a gargoyle!

Screaming at the top of her lungs, Anne reacted on pure instinct, as she grabbed a pillow and shoved it into the gargoyle's face. Shrieking, the monster threw up its terrible talons, then hissing in anger, it tore into the pillow, instantly reducing it to ribbons.

Again Anne screamed . . . and screamed . . . and screamed.

CHAPTER FOURTEEN

J ust as the creature raised its claw to strike again, the door burst open and two people wearing white lab coats ran into the room. One was Dr. Kavathis, who stopped dead in her tracks when she saw the pieces of foam rubber from Anne's pillow scattered all over the room. The other physician was a bearded, bookish-looking man Anne knew as Dr. Dornan. Totally aghast, he just stood there with his mouth hanging open.

"Anne, are you all right?" Dr. Kavathis shouted, now running toward the bed. "What happened to your pillow!"

Startled, the gargoyle turned toward the two doctors, and while its attention was diverted, Anne quickly rolled off the bed and took cover beneath the mattress.

"It's another gargoyle!" she screamed, cowering with her arms over her head. "Watch out! It's sitting right on my bed!"

Then she remembered that she and her parents had decided not to mention anything about her invisible "friends" to the medical staff so as not to distract them from their work. As a result, both Dr. Kavathis and Dr. Dornan didn't have the slightest idea what Anne was talking about. Cackling at the dumbfounded expressions worn by the two doctors, the gargoyle spread its wings and flew straight toward them.

"Ahhh!" Dr. Dornan shrieked as the unseen beast brutally slammed into his chest, then cut three deep, bloody gashes into his right cheek.

Dr. Kavathis, still clueless, screamed as well, then began swinging her arms blindly through the air, hoping to fend off whatever it was that had just injured her colleague.

"It's a monster! It's invisible just like me!" Anne shouted, trying to get Dr. Dornan and Dr. Kavathis to understand what they were up against. But there was little the two physicians could do even if they had understood what Anne was trying to tell them. With their inability to see their attacker, the doctors were no match for the powerful flying monster waging war on them.

The gargoyle, obviously getting a kick out of toying with the helpless humans, continued to circle above their heads, taking an occasional swipe at their faces with its hawklike talons.

Peering out from under the bed, Anne suddenly saw something that gave her hope. A large, red fire extinguisher was hanging on the nearby wall.

Try to think of yourself as a stove, her father had told her. *When you put a pan on a burner, the pan gets hot. But when you take the pan off the stove, it eventually cools back down.*

Remembering her father's words, Anne wondered if coldness could affect invisibility, the way water can put out a fire. If so, the frigid gas in the extinguisher might be an effective weapon against the gargoyle.

There's only one way to find out, she thought, as she scrambled out from under the bed.

The moment the gargoyle saw Anne, it turned its attention away from the panicked scientists, and flew straight in her direction. But unlike either Dr. Kavathis or Dr. Dornan, Anne could see the beastie, and she managed to duck out of its way before it could strike her. While the monster circled around for another pass, she grabbed the extinguisher and yanked it off the wall. Then, as the gargoyle let loose a bloodcurdling shriek, it dived straight for her face.

But Anne was ready. She swung the heavy metal extinguisher at just the right moment and it connected directly with the monster's ugly face. Stunned, the gargoyle dropped limply to the floor.

Trembling from head to toe, Anne fumbled with the extinguisher's trigger as the gargoyle started to get back on its feet. Then she aimed the plastic, cone-shaped exhaust nozzle straight at its ghoulish head.

"Take this!" she snarled, pulling the trigger.

But nothing happened. Terrified, Anne frantically tried again, but not so much as a hiss of air escaped from her weapon.

Could the extinguisher be empty? she thought in a panic.

And then the gargoyle struck.

CHAPTER FIFTEEN

A split second before the gargoyle's razor-sharp talons dug into Anne's flesh, she saw a small ring-shaped pin sticking out of the fire extinguisher's trigger mechanism. *A safety pin!* her mind screamed. Then, gritting her teeth, she yanked the pin free, turned the nozzle toward the gargoyle, and squeezed the spring-loaded trigger with all her might.

Shrieking with evil delight, the beast unwittingly dove straight into the powerful blast of frigid carbon dioxide, and instantly a thin layer of white, glittery frost formed over its entire body. Startled by this unexpected assault, the gargoyle missed Anne by several inches, then was forced to retreat to the far side of the room as she continued to blast it with an unrelenting stream of frigid gas.

Now, to Anne's amazement, the carbon dioxide seemed to be doing more than just coating the monster with ice. It actually seemed to be weakening it! Gasping hoarsely, the monster struggled to stay aloft. But it was losing the battle, and it ultimately dropped to the floor in a defeated heap and curled into a shivering ball.

Standing over the pathetic creature, Anne was joined by Dr. Dornan and Dr. Kavathis, staring wide-eyed at the hideous abomination before them.

"What is that awful thing?" Dr. Kavathis grunted.

Anne perked up. "You mean, you can see it?"

"Yeah, we both can see it," Dr. Dornan reported. "Although I wish we couldn't."

Immediately, Anne shoved the extinguisher at Dr. Kavathis. "Here," she said. "Spray me!"

"Spray you?" the confused physician asked.

"If I'm right, the carbon dioxide in that extinguisher should make me visible," Anne explained. "At least for a while, anyway."

Dr. Kavathis took the canister, which appeared to be floating in the air before her, and backed a few steps away from where she assumed Anne to be.

"Wait!" Dr. Dornan cried. "Will it hurt her?"

"It shouldn't," Dr. Kavathis stated. "It's just carbon dioxide." She then turned toward Anne. "Close your eyes and hold your breath."

Anne did as Dr. Kavathis ordered. A moment later, she was hit in the face with a blast of wet, frigid air. She shivered involuntarily as Dr. Kavathis sprayed the damp carbon dioxide up and down her legs and arms, then across her upper body.

Finally, the doctor released the trigger. "Oh, my!" she gasped. "Well, Anne, welcome back to the world!"

Anne opened her eyes, looked down at her body, and saw herself covered in a thin film of sparkling frost. Then she held up her hands to her face, and for the first time in days saw her skin through the layer of shimmering vapor. "It worked!" she cried.

Excited beyond words, Anne dashed over to a mirror on the wall and stared at herself in wonder. It was true. She was all there. Her eyes. Her mouth. Her cheeks. Her hair. She'd been right! The coldness had neutralized her invisibility field . . . but for how long?

Leaping around the room for joy, Anne suddenly stood dead still when she heard a bestial whine coming from the corner of the room. Spinning around, she saw that the gargoyle was regaining consciousness. Already, the layer of frozen carbon dioxide was beginning to evaporate, and the creature's body was starting to go back to its normal transparent state.

"Hurry, Dr. Kavathis!" Anne shouted. "Blast it!"

Without a moment's hesitation, Dr. Kavathis turned to the monster and gave it another long, hard blast of carbon dioxide. Unable to fight the cold air, the gargoyle wheezed, then fell back limply to the floor.

"You need to get it in a cage while you can still see it," Anne insisted.

"Right," Dr. Dornan said, heading for the door. "I'll get one of the cages from the animal lab."

Five minutes later, the gargoyle was imprisoned in a nine-cubic-foot barred container which, at Anne's suggestion, was to be taken straight to the cafeteria's refrigerated food locker. Dr. Dornan was just carrying the little monster out of Anne's room when Dr. and Mrs. Felcher came running in.

"We just heard what happened in here," Anne's father said excitedly. "Anne, are you—?"

He stopped and stared in wonder as he saw his daughter standing ghostlike before him. As he reached out to touch her, the last of the frozen carbon dioxide evaporated, and she disappeared from view.

"Oh, Anne," her mother moaned in despair. "When is this all going to be over?"

"It's all right, Mom," Anne assured her. "We figured out that cold can short-circuit my invisibility field. Now we just have to make it last."

"That's wonderful!" her father explained, then quickly calmed down. "Not that you're going to have to live in a freezer the rest of your life, sweetheart, but at least this new information gives us a direction in which to work. With luck, it'll just be a matter of time before you're completely back to normal!"

CHAPTER SIXTEEN

"We're at T-minus two minutes and counting," the female technician with the fiery red hair announced as Anne stood anxiously before the open door of the photon refraction chamber. "All systems are ready to go."

For the past three days, periodic blasts of frozen carbon dioxide had kept Anne semi-visible to the doctors and scientists at the Johnston & MacNamara labs as they furiously worked to solve the problem of her seemingly permanent invisibility. After living like a ghost, it had been a relief for Anne to finally be able to talk to people and actually have them look her straight in the eye. However, now that the scientists were going to try to neutralize her invisibility field altogether, the carbon dioxide treatments had stopped, and she had returned to her former transparent state. As a result, people were again moving about her without even acknowledging her existence. Anne found this very unsettling, and she was growing more and more impatient as she waited to become visible again—permanently.

Dr. Felcher, looking tired and worn from having worked forty-eight hours straight, reached out and found his daughter's shoulders, then gave them an encouraging squeeze. "I really think this is going to work, sweetheart," he said, his voice hoarse and full of fatigue. "The results of the computer simulation were very promising."

Dr. Felcher had already spent a great deal of time talking to Anne about what they were about to do. He used terms like "negative field modulations," "anti-proton injections," and "quantum variances," none of which Anne even pretended to understand. All she knew was that the process had something to do with exposing her to temperatures close to zero for a fraction of a second, and that if it worked, she'd emerge from the chamber a normal, completely visible girl.

"We're ninety seconds away!" the red-haired technician announced from the control level above. "Better get a move on into that chamber, hon."

"Everything's going to be fine," Anne's father said. He leaned forward, trying to give Anne a kiss on her cheek, but when he realized he didn't know where her cheek was he just smiled uncomfortably.

Anne gave her father a hug, then stepped into the refraction chamber. The instrument package that had stood here when her science class came to visit nearly two weeks earlier had long since been removed. Now it was just her and the four walls inlaid with their thin metallic strips.

A siren sounded and a yellow warning light began flashing overhead. Dr. Felcher stepped aside as the chamber's heavy door slowly began to swing shut.

Standing in the middle of the chamber, Anne was watching the door close when suddenly she heard a woman scream somewhere outside. Then there was another shout—it was a man this time—followed by what sounded like the crash of furniture.

Instantly, the tone of the siren changed—now it sounded more like an emergency alarm—and the warning light switched from yellow to red.

"Dad! Is something wrong?" Anne called out.

Bolting for the door, which, because of the alarm, had stopped moving, Anne instantly squeezed through the gap. Then, once she was outside the chamber, she realized why her father hadn't answered her. He was lying on the floor against the wall, his face bleeding from several deep gashes in his cheek, a stunned look in his eyes.

"Dad!" Anne raced over to his side. "What happened to you?"

"I—I don't know . . ." he said, his voice coming in weak gasps. "Something hit me . . . I—I didn't see it coming, and then . . ."

All of a sudden, Anne heard a cry as piercing as a vulture's. A second later, she heard another set of screams above her. *Human* screams!

"Don't move," she told her father. Then, before he could protest, she made a dash for the nearby stairs. The screams had come from the control room. Something awful was happening up there.

CHAPTER SEVENTEEN

When Anne reached the control room, she saw in an instant that the scientists and engineers were under attack. Sitting in their chairs, lying on the floor, and backed up against their control consoles, the frightened men and women were wildly batting their arms through the air, desperately trying to protect themselves against vicious enemies they couldn't even see.

But Anne sure saw them. They were gargoyles—four of them—and they were back with a vengeance.

One of the furry beasts landed on the back of a technician and dug its talons into his shoulders. The terrified man screamed and crashed to the floor. Across the room, another one of the winged monsters took a swipe at one of the computer consoles, knocking the terminal to the ground amidst an explosion of sparks and flames.

Horrified, Anne realized that if this assault was allowed to go on much longer, the entire lab could be destroyed, and she'd be trapped in her invisible nightmare forever. She had to do something—and do it fast!

"Hey! Ugly!" Anne shouted. "Over here!"

Amazingly, all four gargoyles instantly stopped their destruction. Then they turned and looked straight at Anne.

"Why don't you pick on someone who can see you?" she taunted. "You think you're so tough, how about coming after me?"

The gargoyles looked at each other curiously, broke into evil smiles, then turned back to Anne.

Uh-oh, she thought. *Now what am I going to do?* Having only a vague plan in mind, Anne spun about and leaped down the steep metal staircase directly behind her. The next moment, the gargoyles launched themselves through the air, dived over the stairway landing, and went rocketing down toward the next level like four huge birds of prey.

Running past her father into the chamber, Anne yelled out to him, "Dad! Close the door behind me— but not until I tell you to!"

"Wh-what?" Dr. Felcher asked, totally confused. He had just managed to pull himself back to his feet when he felt his invisible daughter thunder past him. A split second later, several more invisible beings flew by the befuddled scientist, and he could only guess what they might be.

"Now!" Anne screamed. "Close the door now!"

Realizing what his daughter had in mind, Dr. Felcher lumbered over to the refraction chamber's control panel and punched in the code that canceled the emergency shutdown and resumed the automatic sequencer.

Anne, now back inside the refraction chamber with the four ghoulish gargoyles, threw herself to the hard, metal floor. Then, with nothing to protect herself, she curled into a ball and covered her head with her hands.

Shrieking with evil joy, the frightening foursome flew around the tight, enclosed space preparing to deliver their death blow when . . . *thunk!* The chamber door slammed shut. For an instant, the creatures halted and turned back to see that their one escape route had just disappeared. In that same instant, an expression that might be interpreted as fear—if gargoyles can feel such an emotion—appeared on their nasty little faces.

"Hurry, Dad!" Anne cried. "Hurry!"

Back outside, Dr. Felcher knew exactly what he had to do. As fast as his battered body would carry him, he scrambled up the ladder to the control room where the other members of his team were just beginning to recover from the gargoyle assault. Frantically, he checked a computer monitor and saw that the countdown had resumed, but a full fifteen seconds remained before the computer automatically activated the anti-refraction field. Knowing that there was no way Anne could last even a short period of time inside the refraction chamber with those terrible beasts, he gruffly pushed aside the red-haired scientist and quickly typed a command on her keyboard. A moment later, the nearby monitor screens flashed with a new set of readings, and the sound of roaring generators filled the air.

Meanwhile, sealed inside the refraction chamber with four of the most awful creatures imaginable, Anne screamed in mortal terror as one of the monsters landed on her back. She was sure her life was over when suddenly a high-pitched whine cut through the air and glowing balls of light whirled about the room. Instantly Anne felt every inch of her skin tingle as strange, unknown energies coursed through her body. Above her, the gargoyles howled in agony as their bodies writhed and undulated under this unexpected assault from modern science.

"All right, Dad!" Anne cried as she watched the gargoyles dissolving away like sugar cubes in a glass of water. It seemed that the same energies that were pulling her back into the visible world were simultaneously forcing the gargoyles—who naturally had a vastly different molecular structure than humans—out of their invisible world . . . and into nothingness.

After a few moments, the terrible creatures had completely disintegrated, and only their anguished cries filled the air. Finally, the cries faded as well, and the chamber fell silent, except for the sound of generators winding down.

Sighing with relief, Anne slowly felt the tingling sensation in her skin disappearing. But now her entire body was filled with a new sensation—she felt cold. Terribly, terribly cold.

Shivering uncontrollably as every muscle in her body seemed to go into painful spasm, she wanted desperately to scream for help, but she couldn't even move her mouth to form the words.

Moments later, she heard a low, mechanical hum, and a shaft of brilliant light nearly blinded her as the chamber's door swung open. Squinting, she saw several shadowy figures standing in the doorway. Two of them moved slowly forward, then dropped toward her. Could they be more gargoyles who had come to finish her off?

"Anne!" cried the first figure, whose voice she immediately recognized as her mother's. "Darling, say something. Are you all right?"

"It's over, Anne," said her father, as he, too, knelt down beside her. "You're back."

Her teeth chattering, Anne tried to pull herself out of her fetal position and reach out toward her mother. It was then that she saw something that caught her completely by surprise. It was her own arm, finally whole and solid.

A smile formed on her bluish lips, and a tear rolled down her numb, ivory cheek. As she found comfort in the warmth of her father's embrace, she realized that, at long last, this "ghost" had finally come back to the land of the living.

CHAPTER EIGHTEEN

"Are you sure you had the measles?" Judy Slocum asked in disbelief as she and Anne sat together eating lunch in the junior high cafeteria. "I thought they had vaccines for that or something."

"Well, I guess it was some kind of rare form," Anne managed to say with a perfectly straight face. "Anyway, it really knocked me out."

"But you're fine now, aren't you?" Judy asked anxiously. "I mean, you're not contagious?"

"Don't worry, Judy, you're perfectly safe," Anne assured her.

Anne and her parents had agreed that she should tell everyone she'd had the measles as soon as she'd been ready to return to school. They knew they needed a plausible explanation for her long absence. In fact, she'd have been out of school even longer if Dr. Kavathis had had her way.

After Anne had emerged from the photon refraction chamber with her body temperature

nearly ten degrees below normal, the Johnston &
MacNamara staff physician had insisted that she
remain in the infirmary for at least another week
for observation. Not only did Dr. Kavathis want to
make sure that the girl's core body temperature
returned to normal—which it did that same day—
but she also wanted to confirm that Anne's
invisibility powers were permanently erased—
which they appeared to be.

But by the fifth day, Anne had become so
restless with her confinement that she threatened
to tell her story to every TV network and big city
newspaper in America if she wasn't immediately
released. Seeing that his daughter was truly back to
her old self, Dr. Felcher agreed to let Anne go home
that very same day.

"So, anyway, what did I miss while I was gone?"
Anne asked Judy, eager to hear the most current
gossip. "Is Tony Gilette seeing anybody yet?"

"Not that I know of," Judy said. "Although, from
the looks of things, just about every girl in school is
after him."

Her heart sinking, Anne sighed and turned to
her lunch. With every girl in school now vying for
Tony's attention, she didn't stand a snowball's
chance in August of getting him to notice her. The
sheer numbers alone made the odds against her
virtually unbeatable. And considering the way she'd

made a fool of herself the one and only time she'd ever had a conversation with him, Anne figured she might as well just put the guy completely out of her mind—as if that were possible.

She was trying to come up with another topic to discuss so she could divert her thoughts away from Tony when someone called out, "Hey, Anne!" from across the crowded lunchroom. Looking up, Anne saw Kara Winowski waving to her from the cafeteria line. Anne waved back, and her friend hurried over, a lunch tray in her hands.

But Kara had taken only a couple of steps when she accidentally bumped into Lisa Connors, who was crossing the cafeteria from the other direction. Within seconds there was a resounding crash as plates, food, and drinks went flying in all directions.

"Oops, sorry," Kara said apologetically.

Lisa, who now was wearing the cafeteria's special "mystery" meatloaf on the front of her blue designer sweater, was positively livid. "You clumsy idiot!" she bellowed. "Look what you did to me! You're gonna pay, Winowski!"

Seeing that Kara was in trouble, Anne jumped to her feet and raced over to intervene. "Hey, Lisa, calm down," she said, getting between the two girls. "It's just a few spots, and Kara said she was sorry."

"She doesn't know the meaning of the word sorry," Lisa said, still seething. "When I'm through

THE LIVING GHOST

with her, she's going to wish she was never born. You got a problem with that, Felcher?"

"I just want us all to get along," Anne replied. "How 'bout I treat you to lunch? It's on me."

"Oh, no you don't!" Lisa said, motioning Anne back. "You're not going to pull that trick on me!"

Warily backing away, Lisa didn't see the puddle of tangled spaghetti on the floor, and when her foot hit the sauce, her legs went flying out from under her as though she'd slipped on a patch of ice. Screaming, she went crashing to the floor, landing with a splat directly atop the pile of gooey pasta.

"Have it your way," Anne said with a shrug. She grabbed Kara's arm, and together they raced across the cafeteria accompanied by wild cheers and gales of laughter.

Tony Gilette was waiting at their table when they got there. "Hi, Anne," he said, fixing his gorgeous brown eyes on her.

"Tony?" Anne replied in disbelief.

"I, uh, just wanted to say, welcome back," he said somewhat self-consciously.

"Thanks," Anne replied. "It's good to be back."

"I think it was really cool the way you handled Lisa Connors over there," he said, pointing to Lisa, now running frantically from the cafeteria with a huge red tomato sauce stain on the seat of her pants. "She and her friends are such a bunch of snobs."

Anne found she was unable to disagree. As she searched for something halfway intelligent to say, Tony finally bailed her out. "You know, I hear you're really good in science," he said. "I thought maybe you could help me with my homework after school. We could go over to Marty's Diner and I could buy you a soda or something. If that's okay with you."

Anne couldn't believe what she was hearing. Even with every girl at Thomas Jefferson Junior High at his beck and call, Tony Gilette actually seemed to want to get together with her!

"Yeah, I'd like that," Anne heard herself saying, her voice sounding confident and sure.

"Great," Tony said, looking very relieved. "I'll see you at the bus stop."

"Great," Anne said with a smile.

"Great," Tony repeated. Then, flashing Anne a killer grin, he turned and sauntered off.

"Way to go, Anne!" Judy said, flashing her friend a smile and a big thumbs-up.

"It couldn't have happened to a nicer girl," Kara said wistfully. "Unless, of course, it was me!"

At that same moment, Anne felt a strange breeze brush the back of her neck. It occurred to her that, even now, other gargoyles were still out there, unseen by humans as they went about their eternal mischief. She'd had a brief glimpse into their strange, invisible world, and she had no desire to go back. In fact, she was determined to forget all about them, pretend they didn't exist, and simply go about her business like everyone else.

For right now, her "business" was continuing her lunch with her friends. And so, momentarily gripping her grandmother's ivory cameo, Anne Felcher sat down next to Judy and Kara—pausing only briefly when a salt shaker fell over, seemingly of its own accord, and she heard in the distance a high-pitched laugh.